"I've never met anyone like you."

Claire blinked and then her eyes widened. She drew a deep breath, straightened up and stared wide-eyed at him a moment before her gaze lowered to his mouth.

Jake's heart thudded and he wondered whether she was going to kiss him.

She stepped away from him, leaving more space between them. "I don't know why the attraction, or whatever it is, happens between us," she whispered as if to herself, but he heard her.

"I don't know either, but we might be really missing something if we let what we feel go by without acknowledging it and acting on it. My reaction to you is unique in my life. I'd wager my ranch that your reaction to me is unique in yours, too."

"That doesn't make it good."

"I'm sure it's something that shouldn't be ignored."

* * *

One Wild Texas Night by Sara Orwig is part of the Return of the Texas Heirs series.

Dear Reader,

Welcome to *One Wild Texas Night*, the second book about handsome, successful Texas ranchers who are also family. This is Jake Reed's story. When the story opens, Jake has been out with cowboys who work for him, rounding up livestock to move to a safer part of the ranch because of a raging wildfire.

As Jake drives along the border of his ranch, he sees someone across the fence, and the fire burns dangerously close. While the fire rages behind his neighbor, Jake risks his life, running to yell at her.

Claire is embarrassed that she got into the dangerous situation, and she knows she owes her life to her worst enemy, a man her entire family hates. Since her home is in the fire's path, Jake feels compelled to invite her to stay at his ranch. Claire knows that his offer of a place to stay may be her only hope, so she accepts.

Shocking each of them, a hot, intense attraction springs up between them. Both fight the attraction because they and their families are lifelong enemies, but the fiery appeal is impossible to resist. Their first kiss sets them ablaze. As they have to stay together until she can rebuild, both battle the attraction that is far stronger than their families' century-old feud.

I hope you enjoy *One Wild Texas Night*, the second story of the Texas cousins.

Sara Orwig

SARA ORWIG

ONE WILD TEXAS NIGHT

HARLEQUIN® DESIRE™

Recycling programs for this product may not exist in your area.

ISBN-13: 978-1-335-20933-7

One Wild Texas Night

Copyright © 2020 by Sara Orwig

This edition published by arrangement with Harlequin Books S.A.

For questions and comments about the quality of this book, please contact us at CustomerService@Harlequin.com.

Harlequin Enterprises ULC
22 Adelaide St. West, 40th Floor
Toronto, Ontario M5H 4E3, Canada
www.Harlequin.com

Printed in U.S.A.

Married to the guy she met in college, *USA TODAY* bestselling author **Sara Orwig** has three children and six grandchildren. Sara has published 109 novels. One of the first six inductees into the Oklahoma Professional Writers Hall of Fame, Sara has twice won Oklahoma Novel of the Year. Sara loves family, friends, dogs, books, beaches and Dallas, Texas.

Visit her Author Profile page at Harlequin.com, or saraorwig.com, for more titles.

You can also find Sara Orwig on Facebook, along with other Harlequin Desire authors, at Facebook.com/harlequindesireauthors!

With love to David.

One

Jake Reed's pickup bounced as he sped across an open field on his Texas ranch. Nearby, cowboys on horseback herded his cattle toward the east side of his ranch while a huge wildfire swept the area to the west. None of the noise of cowboys yelling, frightened cattle on the move and Jake's and other cowboys' pickups could drown out the crackle of burning branches, the snap of tree limbs and the occasional crash of a falling tree.

As fire consumed the dry February grass, billowing gray smoke spread overhead, obliterating sunshine. Mesquite vanished in the swift-moving fire. A plane circled above, and Jake glanced at the screen he had set up in his pickup. Hap Green, one of his hands, was flying around overhead with a camera, relaying pictures of the fire to Jake's screen. The pictures confirmed that his house was safe right now—a huge relief. They had radio communication also, so Jake could ask questions.

As long as the wind held in the west, Jake knew his house wouldn't be in danger. Even now, as the wind began to shift from the north, his ranch house would remain out of the fire's path. His house was far to the east, but he knew how fast fires spread and how easily a tiny spark from a burning cedar could blow, land on a roof and ignite a house, so he remained vigilant. He and some of his men had plowed a large area on two sides of his house, as well as around the outbuildings and other homes. They had dug what was, hopefully, too big an area for the fire to jump, but if the wind kept shifting, nothing would be safe.

He saw the barbed wire fence separating his land from that of his feuding neighbor—a Blake. Both families had fought since they had settled in Texas after the Civil War more than a century and a half ago. He felt a jolt of surprise when he glanced across the fence and saw someone kneeling on the ground by an animal.

He turned his pickup to drive closer, and in seconds he saw it was his neighbor Claire Blake. The solitary Blake living in the area, she owned the family ranch now. Even though he saw her at cattle auctions, rodeos, the bank and grocery in Persimmon, Texas, their nearest small town, they hadn't really spoken in years—except when they had gone to court to fight each other.

He motioned to one of his men to keep going forward, and then he continued to the fence. Her pickup was parked too far away for her to get to it quickly, and she had her back to the fire—unwise with a fast-moving blaze in high wind.

Her grandfather had brought in Texas red cedars as a windbreak. Big mistake in Jake's view. They turned out to be nuisance trees, gobbling up groundwater, spreading rapidly and defying control, and he fought constantly to keep them off his land. Now the fire was sweeping through them on her ranch, each cedar exploding in flames when mere sparks touched it, the blaze spreading faster than a man could run.

If she didn't get out in the next few minutes, she wasn't going to get out alive. Even though the Reeds had a long history of fighting the Blakes, he couldn't leave her to burn. He remembered that Sunday when he had been driving past her church and he'd seen her laughing with a companion. She'd looked so attractive that if she had been anybody else except a Blake, he would have approached her. She was never with her brothers, Clyde and Les, who had caused a lot of trouble for his dad when they were growing up with mischief that they called harmless pranks. Claire lived alone out on the family ranch, and none of her family ever came to see her. Maybe she couldn't get along with her brothers any more than most of the other people in the area. Still, she was a Blake, and probably as annoying as the rest of her family. He didn't speak to her and she didn't speak to him. Despite all that, he increased his speed, bouncing over the rough ground toward her and the raging fire.

She was kneeling over an animal—a dog, he saw now—with her pickup a hundred yards behind her, too near a stand of cedars and native oaks, too near the fire. The minute he stepped out of his truck, he looked up, turning to face the wind.

The wind was changing directions—no surprise—but it was what he had been praying wouldn't happen, and it was going to be deadly. More of his land would burn now. He knew from flying over their ranches that if the wind came fully out of the north, her home would be engulfed. And right now, they, as well as the dog, were in the fire's path. Still bending over the dog, she seemed totally oblivious. He was surprised, because the general consensus in the area was that she seemed to be a good rancher. He yelled, but the fire and wind drowned out his call.

He leaned down, pulling the barbed wire strands wide enough to step between them, avoiding the barbs while going through the fence quickly, then ran toward her.

"Hey!" he yelled again, and when she looked up,

she jumped to her feet and stepped back as if he was a threat. Damn. He was risking his life for her, and she'd better not fight him about going with him.

Claire Blake looked up from the birthing dog before her, glanced over her shoulder and was startled to see her neighbor waving his arms and running toward her. Even though he was handsome as the devil, he was from a family that might as well have been related to Satan himself. Whatever he wanted, he'd better leave her alone, which he always had in the past. For a moment, she wondered if this was his dog and she had wandered onto her land to have her pups. No matter. She didn't have to do one thing Jake Reed said. All she had to do was take care of the dog and the five newborn pups in front of her, because they were in danger from the fire. She turned back to look at the dog spread on a blanket in front of her and the tiny newest pup in her hands as she cleaned the little wrinkled brown Lab puppy, its eyes still tightly closed. Thankfully, for her and the exhausted new mom in front of her, this was the last.

She knew the fire raged behind her and they had to get out. Would Jake help her with the pups? No, she had never counted on anything from him, and she wouldn't start now. If the situation had been reversed, her brothers wouldn't have helped him. She had to get the dogs out on her own.

"Queenie, you picked a lousy time to have your

babies." She didn't know the dog's real name, so she gave her a temporary one. "We've got to get out of here. I wouldn't blame you, but please don't bite my neighbor." She ran her hand over the dog's head, and Queenie's tail thumped.

"You've got to go," Jake Reed yelled as he ran toward her.

"Duh," she mumbled. "I know we need to get out," she said, still working over the dog and pups.

"The wind's changing. You and the dogs will burn," he yelled. As he drew closer, she stood and faced him. Even under the circumstances, the thought crossed her mind when she saw her neighbor that he really was the best-looking guy in the next six counties.

She dragged her eyes from him, and for the first time in a while, she glanced at the fire. Shock chilled her, driving all other thoughts from her mind. The fire had changed direction and was nearly upon them. It seemed just minutes ago she had looked at it and deemed them out of immediate danger. Then she turned to Jake. So, what was he doing here? Coming to save her? She couldn't believe that. No, the dog must be his. "I didn't notice how fast the fire is moving. I need to get the dogs into my pickup. If I take—" She gasped as her eyes lit on her vehicle. "Oh no."

"I'd forget that one," he remarked, stopping near

her as flames engulfed her pickup. "I'll get mama dog. Grab the pups and let's go."

"My pickup…it was fine a moment ago," she said, not sure what shocked her more—her destroyed truck or the fact that he was offering to get her out of the area.

"Is this your dog?" she asked him.

"Hell, no. Let's go," he ordered, picking up the dog. "Grab the pups and get into my truck. Move it," he snapped. "Your pickup is toast. We're next. Go, dammit."

"I had no idea—" She realized she had been too focused on the dogs and had made what could have been a fatal error in ignoring the fire for a few minutes. That sent shivers all over her.

"Put some pups on her so she doesn't think we're taking them away from her," he said. Claire quickly placed three pups on the mother.

"C'mon, move," he shouted over his shoulder. "We've got to get out of here while we can."

His brisk order cut through her shock, and she grabbed up the remaining pups and rushed after him as he ran for his pickup. She glanced back once, and even in the heat of the raging inferno, sweat running down her face and body, she was chilled.

As he ran ahead of her, his long legs covering the ground easily, she realized she owed her life to him. Her worst enemy. He had rescued her and the dogs from dying in the inferno. How would she ever repay him when she didn't even like to speak to him and rarely ever had? She had made a terrible error in turning her back on the fire, but she'd made just as big a mistake in getting into a predicament where her rescuer was Jake Reed. A lifelong enemy of her and every member of her family. How was she going to cope with the fact that he had just saved her life? Just as bad—how was she going to cope with the nagging awareness of how appealing and sexy he was?

Two

Jake could feel the heat and hear the roar of the fire and the constant snap and crackle behind them as cedars exploded, consumed by flames.

Sweat ran down his face and back from the fire's heat. It was the middle of February with warm Texas winds blowing, spreading the fire and fanning the flames. Trees ignited and burned instantly while the dry winter grass fueled the intense fire.

At the fence, he held the dogs closer against his chest and then he jumped the wire. Carrying the pups in a bandanna, Claire slipped between fence strands and caught up with him.

In minutes he had the mother dog and pups in the back of his pickup on a blanket.

"I'll ride with them," Claire said, turning to climb into the back. He took her arm, and the minute he touched her, she looked up at him. For an instant he was lost in big, thickly lashed green eyes that made him forget danger, fire, circumstances, everything except his neighbor and worst enemy only inches away with her wide eyes focused on him. A tree crashed and shook him into awareness of his surroundings again.

"She's fine. Get inside," he ordered. "Hurry." He dashed around to get in, starting the engine as she climbed in beside him. He turned his pickup away from the fire that was only yards behind them now. When the wind changed direction, the fire had begun to fan out. The blaze picked up force, and more cedars burst into flames behind them.

She twisted to look back and shivered. "You saved us. If you hadn't yelled, I wouldn't have made it out. The dogs wouldn't have, either."

Jake glanced in his rearview mirror. Thank heavens he had almost every cedar on his place dug up. Some had gone to businesses and places in town that wanted them. Others had just been cut up for posts or firewood.

He glanced at her; she wrapped her arms around herself as if she trembled. It shocked him that she had been so oblivious to the fire, because she ran her ranch by herself and he'd always thought of her as competent. It also shocked him that he had just saved her life—his biggest enemy. Actually, her family and her no-good brothers were the really bad ones. But she was blood kin to them and had grown up with them, so she was bound to be just like them. Even if it had been her rotten brothers in danger, he couldn't have gone off and let them burn. He was glad they'd saved the dog and pups, too. He couldn't have left them, either.

While he drove swiftly away from her property, the pickup bounced roughly. He didn't care. All he wanted to do was get more distance between them and the fire that was traveling with lightning speed now. He knew how easily they could get trapped in a ring of flames.

"Are you okay?" he asked after a few more minutes when he finally felt he could slow down.

"No. I'm not okay," she snapped. "I know what I'm losing," she answered, but he was relieved that her voice was firm, and she didn't sound on the verge of losing her composure. "I really let down my guard. I made a major mistake by not watching the fire and getting out of there sooner. It really shakes me up when I pull some bonehead stunt running this ranch. This time, if not for you, my mistake would have been my last."

She looked back over her shoulder. "I'm still worried about the dogs bouncing around back there. They don't know they're being rescued."

"Don't worry about the dogs. They'll be fine, and we're getting them to safety with us. And you did cut it too close, but we all make mistakes. Don't ever turn your back on a wildfire except to get away from it."

Her phone buzzed, and she answered. At the same time, he received a call. It took only seconds for his call. When he finished, he saw her call had ended.

"That was the sheriff," he said. "They're telling everyone to evacuate this area. I need to get all my hands out," he said, calling his foreman.

"Just before you appeared, I had the same call from one of the deputies. My place is in the fire's path. I've already told all my people to get out, but I'm checking anyway." She made a call.

When the fire had started, Jake had had the foresight to get his livestock moved. Now that the wind had shifted out of the north, driving the fire across her ranch and more of his, he was glad he'd done that and relieved his house was far to the east and out of the fire's path, though some of his acreage was sure to burn.

"I'm sorry you're taking a direct hit. That fire's going right across your place."

She twisted in the seat to look behind her. "I'm going to lose my house and everything in it," she said so softly he barely heard her, and this time he noticed the waver in her voice. He glanced in his rearview mirror to determine they were leaving the fire behind. Then he slowed and stopped, letting the motor run. She was turned away from him, her shoulders slightly hunched.

"Well, this is a first for more than a century—a Reed and a Blake together without fighting," he said, more to himself than her. "I'm sorry about your ranch. That's a tough one," he said, meaning it. He didn't like her or her family. He didn't know her, but he knew her rotten brothers and had fought the older two in schoolyard fights, played against them in football and witnessed their hijinks enough to know he really didn't like them or their dad.

She turned to look at him and he gazed into those big emerald-green eyes again, with long, dark brown lashes that needed no makeup to be beautiful. That thought shocked him. Her skin was flawless. She was tan from being outside. Her dark red hair was in a thick braid that hung down her back. Her lips were full, red and appealing. Her mouth looked soft, kissable. With a jolt, he realized where his thoughts were going. Of all the women on the earth, this was the one he did not want to find highly appealing or start fantasizing about. Then he remembered the fire and how she was going to lose her home and her belongings.

"I know we've been enemies all our lives and have never even said a civil word to each other before, but

I'm sorry you're going to lose your house," he said, surprised at himself, because he had had some bitter courtroom fights with her over ranch disagreements. "That's tough."

"Thank you," she whispered, looking down and turning her head slightly. "It hurts." She was silent a moment, and so was he.

"You may not really know much about me," she said in a low voice and then hesitated. He thought she wasn't going to say anything else, but then she started again. "Long ago, I lost everything important to me except the ranch," she said softly. "My maternal grandfather owned the ranch, as you know. My dad and my brothers never liked it, and my grandfather gave it to me. Now I'm going to lose my home, and then all I'll have is the land and my livestock. Sometimes a person needs more than land and livestock," she whispered. "I'm sorry, but this has been tough, and I don't see any improvement looming."

She ran her fingers lightly across her eyes. He felt sorry for her because her father and brothers never came back to the area, and her mother had died years earlier. She had a sister, but she and Jake's brother had been a closed chapter since the year they had married and run away. For a moment he thought of the secrets he knew about her family, the ones she didn't know. And never would know. He wondered if she had friends or anybody who cared about her.

Impulsively he put his arm around her shoulders,

the gesture shocking him that he could feel sorry for someone he had disliked for a lifetime. An even bigger shock—she was soft, appealing. He put that out of his mind quickly.

"Sorry. Right now, there's no easy way to stop that damn fire," he said. "That's part of the hazard we face in living out here," he added. The moment he slipped his arm around her and drew her closer, letting her lean against him, awareness of her shook him. She was soft and smelled sweet in spite of being outside and caring for the dogs. She placed one hand against his chest as if to push him away. Only she didn't push in the slightest.

She looked up at him, and he felt enveloped in those big green eyes that stopped his breathing and made his heart pound. A silent protest flitted through his thoughts that he couldn't possibly feel this response to her. He absolutely didn't want to discover that this was the one woman who could make his heart race just by looking at him. All the common sense, caution, generations of fighting between their families, having little more than a dozen civil words spoken between them in their entire lifetimes and those words they'd said in the past few minutes—it all dissipated when he looked into her eyes. He did not want to feel one iota of attraction to her. But he did. And he was absolutely sure that feeling was mutual.

There was no woman in his life right now, but he

needed to get one fast if he was having this kind of reaction to a Blake. They both came from families that hadn't spoken for generations, over a century of animosity, bitter battles from the tales of early-day relatives. At least his relatives had told him plenty. He knew things she didn't. From stories handed down, they each had a legacy of feuding families, with hangings, stabbings, shootings, cattle rustling— all kinds of robberies and torn fences. And now, in his own lifetime, there were still secrets. He wondered about her and her life. She was a neighbor who lived a solitary life. He didn't think she ever went out with anyone or partied or had any social life.

Thoughts of what he should do ran through his mind. Even as those thoughts struck him, he struggled to look away from her big green eyes until his gaze lowered to her mouth. Her full, rosy lips looked incredibly kissable. Oh damn, what a thought. He almost groaned aloud. His gaze flew back to meet hers. When something flickered in the depths of her eyes, he realized he was right. She felt something, too.

Instantly, that knowledge had a double effect— first, he didn't want her to feel anything. Second, the realization that she did feel something made his heart race faster and gave him a more intense awareness of her.

He had seen her, passed her in town, gone to the same school—although at three years older, he had been in a different grade. In the past they had either fought or ignored each other. Until now.

Until today, he'd let his foreman or one of the cowboys handle any problems that had occurred due to their adjoining ranches. They rarely had to talk to one another and that worked for them. Often, she did the same and the two foremen worked things out.

As he glanced again at her and she looked at him, he realized it was the first time he had really noticed her.

How long had he looked at her? A couple of seconds? Ten, fifteen? Whatever time frame, he felt as if his whole life had changed in a subtle but irreversible way. He would never again see her the same way he always had. Worse, right now, he wanted to tighten his arm around her, pull her closer and kiss her. That shocking thought galvanized him to move away, and he released her. Instantly she scooted away, and her cheeks became pink—adding to her beauty. How could she suddenly be appealing? She was a lifelong enemy, as well as an enemy of every relative he had ever had. Generations of relatives over the last century. And now he was caught in a hot attraction? Oh wow, did he need to call someone and go out with a good-looking, fun woman.

When Claire Blake moved away, she looked back at her ranch. "Oh my heavens. My whole ranch is on fire, and now the flames are headed right for my house. From the first moment I heard about this fire, I hoped this wouldn't happen."

He reached in front of her to get two clean bandannas out of the glove compartment. He held one out to her. "Put this on and maybe it'll help filter out the smoke. I'll get us and the dogs away from this."

"Thanks," she said, taking the bandanna to tie it behind her head and over her nose and mouth. It just made him even more aware of her big green eyes. He drew a deep breath, coughed slightly and wished he didn't have any kind of response to her. He never had before today. Now, he knew that no matter what happened between them, he would never again see her in the same impersonal way he always had.

"The sheriff said to evacuate, so that's what we'll do," he said, turning to drive and trying to focus on getting away quickly.

She didn't answer, and he glanced at her. She was looking back, and she ran her hand across her face. He was certain she wiped away tears.

His screen crackled, and his pilot's voice came in. She twisted to look at his screens. "What are those?"

"I can get pictures sent from one of my planes. I have someone flying around, getting those pictures of the fire so I know what's happening. He's flown out of this area now because of the smoke. Even if he could get a picture, I don't think you'd want to see your house."

"No, I really don't."

"Don't worry, he's just taking pictures of my place unless I tell him differently."

She nodded and looked out the window over her shoulder.

Rain was predicted in late afternoon, and he prayed for her sake it arrived sooner. He looked up at the sky, but it was hidden by the smoke spreading in all directions overhead. He knew from flying over their land before that she lived in the original big farm home that was said to be over a century old. It would hurt to lose your house no matter what, but an old one like that would be really tough. It had lasted all these years, but there was no way it would survive this raging, out-of-control wildfire that was consuming everything in its path. He suspected her house was filled with hand-me-downs from generations of her family—heirlooms that she treasured. They wouldn't make it through the fire. He felt sorry for her, which surprised him.

"Claire," he said, her name rolling off his tongue for the first time in his life. He had never called her by her first name, and saying it made him think again of the moment when he had looked into her big eyes and then at her mouth that looked made for kisses. He almost groaned aloud at that one. She was Claire Blake, he reminded himself. A Blake—the despised and hated enemy, including all her rotten relatives, for generations as far back as his family history went.

He didn't think she ever went out with anyone.

She was a loner, staying on her ranch. On Friday or Saturday nights when he was out, he never saw her. He rarely even thought about her and never had wondered why he didn't see her. Now he wondered. And the minute he realized that, he knew he shouldn't. He should go right back to ignoring her and seeing her the way he always had—a neighbor whose entire family had a feud with his family. But he knew he couldn't see her just that way anymore.

Without doing anything except looking at him, she had turned his life topsy-turvy.

She was going to need a place to stay tonight. Within the hour she would be homeless. None of her family lived close now. Her father and brothers had all moved away, but she needed to be out here. She couldn't walk away from her ranch and all the people who worked for her.

He dreaded asking her to stay at his cabin. He liked his privacy, and they were bitter, lifelong enemies. So why was he about to offer her shelter? To get shut up in his cabin with her for an indefinite period of time?

What worried him the most was the unwanted, unreasonable attraction she had stirred. He didn't want to be attracted to a Blake, much less one who was a loner, almost a recluse. He wished he could stop thinking about her appeal, but that was impossible with her sitting close. He didn't want to think about spending the night with her in his cabin or, even worse, maybe a couple of days together. He was sure after a few minutes that unwanted and unreasonable attraction would disappear as swiftly as it had come. But even as that thought ran through his mind, he remembered how soft her lips had looked.

"Claire, I have a cabin on the river about thirty miles from here. It's far enough away to be okay. You can come stay there. It's big. There's plenty of room." Even as he said the words, he hoped she would refuse, but he suspected she had no other choice. Where else could she go?

She glanced up, her eyes widening in surprise, and from the crinkled line around them he knew she was smiling. Just the thought made his insides clench again, causing another worry. If she stayed with him, would he keep having these physical reactions to her?

As a kid, he'd thought she was plain-looking, and he paid little attention to her. She was three years younger, so they were never involved in anything together.

He responded to women, to being with a good-looking woman or a fun woman, but this was a totally unwanted, unpredictable, shocking response to a woman he had spent a lifetime avoiding. Not to mention the hostility between their families and sometimes between them. Something she seemed to have put on hold as much as he had.

"Stay with me," he surprised himself by repeating. "It's a big cabin, and we ought to be able to get through a night or two under the same roof."

A faint smile lit her eyes again and was gone in an instant, but that tiny smile made his heart clench again. What could it mean if he was continually having this intense reaction to his deepest and maybe only enemy? Well, only enemy in the area. Her brothers, who'd moved away, would fall into that category. Just the two older ones, he amended. Her younger brother, Laird, had always stayed out of the fights.

Jake knew that her two older brothers hated him, and the feeling was mutual. Ironically, their reasons were probably as good as his. He didn't want any part of them. They had secrets they tried to hide from everyone. They would be shocked if they ever discovered he knew what they knew.

Years ago, when his brother had eloped with her sister, they'd mostly severed ties with their families so they weren't around, either, though Jake kept in touch with his brother.

If he stopped to think about it, Jake knew a lot about her family, while he suspected she knew almost nothing about his. And he would never tell her what he knew or how he knew it. There were secrets he had promised to keep, and he definitely needed to keep them from her.

"I'm sorry for the circumstances," he said, "but other than my brother and your sister, this is the first time in generations that I know about when a Reed and a Blake have been civil to each other."

"Well, under the circumstances…" She shrugged, and he knew what she meant. Then she looked away. "You saved me and the dogs, and now you're offering me a place to stay… I don't know what to say." He was about to utter *Say yes* when she turned back to him and told him, "Except I'm grateful. I'll go to your cabin. Actually, *we'll* go to your cabin," she added, nodding to the dogs in the back of the truck. "Thank you."

"You're welcome," he said, smiling at her, thinking that was another first in his life in dealing with her. He'd spent too many years fighting with her family to want to become friends with her, and that feeling was mutual, he was sure. So he shifted his gaze to the road ahead of him and dragged his thoughts back to the business at hand. "We're close enough that I can keep tabs on the location of the fire until it's out. It's too close for comfort, that's for sure, and the wind isn't predictable."

"I'm glad I got my animals out and everyone who works for me, and their families are safe and accounted for."

"Amen to that one," he said. "We had good advance notice on this fire." A few minutes of driving later, he said, "I keep the cabin stocked with food because I stay there often to fish, so we'll have plenty to eat."

"At the moment I don't feel like eating. All I can do is think about my house. I have houses on the ranch for several of my employees, too, and when those homes burn, my folks will lose their possessions." He heard her take a deep but shaky breath, and out of the corner of his eye, he saw her brush her fingers over her eyes again.

"I'm sorry, but this hurts. It's just another loss in what seems like a series of them."

He shot her a curious glance, and she went on to explain. "My mom died when I was seven. My big sis took her place and was a second mother until four years later, when she eloped with your brother. They cut all ties, and my sister was another big loss in my life. She left me a letter telling me why she felt they had to cut those ties. Regina was eighteen when she eloped. Now I'm thirty and she's thirty-seven."

Jake recalled that time. His brother had only been twenty-one.

"After they eloped, my dad and brothers weren't exactly sympathetic about my losses." She shook her head and turned to the window, and he figured she was done telling him about her life. But she continued.

"My mother had money of her own from her family. She left that money to Regina as long as she took care of me until I was eighteen. If for any reason she stopped caring for me before I was eighteen, the money went to me, and that's what happened

when she married your brother—a sizable amount of
money went to me. Somehow that money was a buf-
fer between my dad and my sister and later between
my dad, my brothers and me. I think they hoped I
would take care of their bills if they couldn't. Thank
goodness I never did have to."

As she talked, his gaze kept flitting to her. Her
story was sad, but his thoughts were more on her
appearance, those big green eyes that he had never
noticed before. Also her thick red hair, a dark red. It
took an effort to keep his focus on his driving, but
he couldn't stop thinking about her. Idly, he wondered how she would look if she ever let her hair out
of that braid. Startled when he realized his train of
thought, he tried to get his attention back on what
she was saying.

"My dad remarried and moved to south Texas.
Then, when I went to college, I got away from my
brothers and they moved on, too, getting jobs in Dallas and Houston. None of them like ranching, so they
don't come here often. I'm trying to reconnect with
them, but we live far apart, so that makes it difficult."

He was thankful her family didn't come back, but
he didn't say so.

"I wonder if any of my family may see my house
in flames, because this fire is big news, I'm sure."

At the mention of the fire, Jake glanced back at the
screen, at the information and pictures from his pilot.
He was sorry her home was burning, but it wouldn't

change the bitter feud they'd both grown up observing. That wasn't something that would ever change. Every member of his family had fought or had trouble with or just disliked her family, and vice versa. It was the way they were all raised, and it wouldn't ever change. It hadn't changed in the last century and a half, and he saw no earthshaking event, even this fire, that would end the feud. That was impossible. He suspected after today, she would go right back to refusing to speak to him, and he would do the same with her.

Even though he was increasing the distance between them and the fire as he drove, he watched for any new hot spots. So far, so good.

"I've made a life for myself," she continued, "and I love ranching. I love my horses."

"I've seen your horses—you have some fine ones," he said. Yeah, her horses might be great, but her family was lousy. She probably thought the same about his family.

They rode in silence for a few minutes until she started talking again. "I had the house remodeled and have made a home I love, something stable in my life. It's going up in smoke right now, or maybe it's already just ashes," she said in little more than a whisper.

"Claire, you'll rebuild. You've already been through a bunch of disasters and survived. You'll survive this one," he said quietly, amazed he was trying to console a woman who had been an enemy all his life. It still gave him a peculiar feeling to address her by her first name. Up to now, she'd simply been "my enemy neighbor" any time in the past when he had thought about her.

Out of the corner of his eye, he could see that she looked at him intently, and his pulse jumped. Once again, he felt that urge to put his arm around her to console her. And he knew what he wanted was more than consoling her. Glancing at her, he had a sudden urge to reach out and pull the bandanna away so he could let his gaze sweep over her features, and he felt his pulse rev up another notch. When they didn't get along and she was his enemy, how could a mere thought cause this?

When he went out on weekends, he saw gorgeous women, sexy, fun women who flirted with him, and his reaction wasn't as intense as right now with a woman who didn't even like him. They had a truce at the moment, and even if it lasted for a few days or a few weeks, which he seriously doubted, an attraction was impossible. Only it was happening, knotting his insides, making him hot and causing him to want to reach for her to taste those fabulous lips.

It would seem she'd worked some magic spell on him, except she looked as dazed as he felt, and he suspected she definitely didn't want to feel any attraction to him.

His phone buzzed. "Here's my foreman," he said

to her and took the call. When he ended the call, he glanced at her.

"All my people are accounted for and out of here. When we first heard about the fire, we started moving livestock and getting families and their pets off the ranch. I left one bunch of cowboys moving my cattle and was headed to join another when I saw you and the dogs."

At the mention of the animals, she looked over her shoulder at them. Satisfied they were okay, she turned back. "I was the only protection the dogs had. I had to do what I did. But if you hadn't come—" She shook her head. "Well, thanks again for the rescue. You went against all you've been taught, but you saved my life and the dogs. I owe you big-time for that one. In fact, I'll have to be nice to you now," she said, but she sounded as if that was a major calamity.

"I wouldn't leave you or the animals to burn," he answered.

"Frankly, I'm not sure my brothers would have come to your rescue," she admitted. "The feud is still strong in our generation. It isn't ever going away. They always said your great-granddad shot and killed my great-grandfather."

Feeling a little flare of annoyance, Jake shook his head. "My family always said your great-grandfather shot and tried to kill my great-grandfather. And the feud goes further back than those guys. However it went, I couldn't leave anyone behind to burn. Not even your brothers or your dad, in spite of our history. At least I've never shot at your family, and I hope none of you have at us. Just our great-grandparents exchanged gunfire."

"I've been told that, but I didn't know if it was the truth. I figured it was," she said, and he glanced at her to see her studying him. Her bandanna accidently slipped down, and he notice a deep pink in her cheeks, and he wondered what she had been thinking. And he knew he shouldn't speculate on why her cheeks had flushed.

He tried to shift his thoughts to something neutral and impersonal. It was an impossible task with her sitting so close. His reaction to her stunned him. He had seen her off and on all his life, but because she was a Blake, he'd paid little attention to her.

"By the way," she said, turning to him again, "since we are speaking to one another now, I saw in the local paper and in one of the ranch magazines that you're one of four ranchers who have donated large sums to rebuild the old arena that burned in Fort Worth. For years, that was a bitter subject with my family."

"So I've heard. I heard that your family planned to buy the land decades ago when it first came on the market and were going to build something there, but my family slipped in and donated the money to the city for an arena before your family could buy the property."

"That's close to the version I've heard. Maybe a little more cheating by your family to get the city to build an arena. We'll never know," she said, a smile wrinkling her eyes.

"That was all before our time, so we'll never know," he said, but his thoughts were really on her smile that made him want to smile in return. Her eyes seemed to twinkle when she smiled, and it made her even more appealing. *More appealing.* That was staggering. He didn't want to be aware of her at all. Once again, he told himself he needed to get out more. He'd stayed on the ranch the past few weekends. He wasn't going to in the future. Not with this kind of reaction to a Blake.

"I'm glad the arena is being rebuilt. I love rodeos. I loved that arena. Thanks so much to you and your cousins for contributing to build a new one."

"You're welcome. I liked that arena, and so did my cousins and my friends. We all competed there. We wanted to see it rebuilt and continued."

"I don't know your cousins."

"One of them, Cal, contributed to the arena. He worked out of the country, although he owned a Texas ranch. He worked for the government and was killed in an accident. We've asked that they name the arena after him—the Cal Brand Arena."

"I'm so sorry you lost your cousin," she said, sounding as if she meant what she said.

"Thanks. He was a great guy, and we miss him,

even though we didn't see a lot of him these last years."

He appreciated her sympathy and was pleased that she was interested in the arena. "What do you know, we can get along for a few minutes."

She looked startled and nodded. "I hope so," she said quietly, and he wondered if she was thinking about fights they'd had in the past and how cold they had been when they had gone to court with boundary disputes, arguments over water rights and other complaints. They'd never conversed with each other on those occasions. This was a first. He didn't expect this sudden friendliness to last, though. Too much history in their families.

"You've put a good distance between us and the fire now," she noticed. "For a minute there I was worried about us getting away. The fire has to have reached my house by now," she added. She got out her phone and in minutes had news and pictures. "I don't think I'll get a picture of my house because of the smoke. Every once in a while, the wind clears the smoke enough for a picture, but it's just ranch land. I'm not sure I even want to see a picture of my house."

"They're probably getting the pictures from a drone," he stated. "Don't look. It won't help you. We got out with our lives. That's the main thing. Focus on that."

She nodded and turned to look out the back window and watch the fire. "When my sister ran away to marry your brother, she left that letter for me, like I told you. She explained they had to leave because of my father and brothers. I've always kept her letter because that's all I have of her. Now even that has burned and is gone."

He sat quietly, remembering how his brother had told him he would have to disappear because her dad and older brothers would come after them. His brother had shared secrets with him, but her sister hadn't shared any with her, judging from her few remarks. Probably because Claire was only eleven at the time. He had vowed to keep his brother's secrets, and he always had.

His thoughts shifted to the present. He was still shocked he was taking her home with him. They would be under the same roof—his worst enemy in the entire world living in his house, eating with him, talking and getting to know each other. They were acting civil to each other right now, but he knew that was because of the fire and danger and her loss. It was temporary and superficial. They had generations of hatred ingrained into them, and it wasn't going away. He would help her, but he still didn't like her. She had no clothes—nothing, he realized. When he could, he should drive her into Persimmon. She could pick up a few essentials there.

He glanced at her, and at the same time she turned to look at him, and he felt a clutch to his insides.

His truck bounced over a couple of big stones, and he jerked his attention back to the road. He focused on his driving, but surprise over her features stayed with him. He'd always thought her incredibly plain, but he knew it was because of the way she dressed, either in overalls or jeans, with no makeup, her hair in the thick braid that hung down her back. So why was she looking so attractive to him now?

He wished she had refused to stay at his cabin, but she'd probably figured the same as he had—that the only motels anywhere in the vicinity would be totally booked with people driven out by the fires. He had invited her to stay at his place, so he was stuck with her. Too bad it was only a getaway fishing cabin and didn't have all the guesthouses his ranch home did. With them both beneath the same roof, was he even going to be able to tolerate her?

That thought made him grit his teeth. She had grown quiet, and he wondered if she was having the same thoughts about him. He knew she didn't like him and considered him her worst enemy, because she had told him so more than once.

In a short time, they were on a highway heading east. Would thirty miles to the east be safe from the fire? He would just have to keep up with the reports and be aware of the fire and wind conditions. But, for now, they were safe, and he motioned to her that they could finally remove their bandannas.

"We both need to pray for rain," he said, breaking the silence in the truck. "We're supposed to have rain later today, but there's no seeing the sky for all the smoke."

"The rain will be too late for my place," she said in a monotone.

"Sorry. You're right. What about your livestock, cattle and horses? Where'd they go?"

"Do you know Dan Sloan?"

"Sure."

"Yesterday when we got the first warning, Dan contacted me. He sent some men to help and moved my cattle to his place for now. He's down the road to the east—farther east than your ranch, as you know."

"You had to move your livestock around my ranch, then, to get to him. When you move them back, let me know and you can cross my ranch."

With the bandanna now around her neck, she smiled, a big smile that warmed him like sunshine and made his pulse jump.

"Thank you. It will be a lot quicker and easier to cross your land. The Sloans are very nice people," she continued, and he tried to focus on what she was saying.

"They invited me to stay with them, but they already have his brother and his brother's family, which includes five more kids. I didn't want to impose on him, and I don't want to impose on you."

"No need. It'll just be the two of us," he said, and the minute the words were spoken, he felt his breath catch. He had answered matter-of-factly and imper-sonally, but it didn't come out that way.

"...the two of us..."

The words echoed in his mind and sounded far more personal. What kind of chemistry did they have between them? He wouldn't have thought any kind would be possible, but she stirred some responses in him as if she were sitting there flirting with him, which she wasn't at all. Besides, she was as plain as a mud hen. The moment that thought came, he had a vivid memory of her face. He glanced at her again and looked into big, gorgeous green eyes with thick brown lashes and dark red hair. She wasn't as plain as a mud hen at all—she just projected that image until he got up close. That realization shocked him, and he wanted to stop driving and turn and really look at her. He realized how ridiculous that would be. She was a Blake, and he'd better not forget that.

"Damn," he said without realizing he had even spoken aloud until she turned abruptly to stare at him.

"Is something wrong?" she asked, sounding wor-ried.

"Sorry. I was just thinking about the fire and your loss," he lied.

"That's nice of you," she said. "I figured you might not really care, but it's nice to know you do."

He glanced at her again and was caught once more by those gorgeous green eyes. Quickly he turned back to his driving. "Damn," he said again, this time under his breath.

They rode in silence for a while, and then he heard a slight sound from her. He glanced at her and saw that her hands were on her face and she was shaking. He checked the rearview mirror. They had put a big distance between themselves and the fire, so he slowed and cut the engine, turning to put his arm around her lightly.

"Claire, I'm sorry you lost your home," he said, really meaning it, because that would be a devastating loss.

She turned to him, placing her head against his chest as she cried. For an instant she sobbed, but then she got control. With no tissues for her to wipe her face, he held out a clean bandanna. "Here, take this."

She took it and just held it. "You just have an endless supply of bandannas?" she asked, trying to smile. But her smile vanished as she wiped her eyes. "I'm sorry. I feel stupid crying again. It's just that I've lost everything. All my life I've been losing what I love," she said so softly he could barely hear her. "I don't ever want to fall in love, because I'd lose the person I love. I don't even want to get real close to friends any longer. I'm glad I still have my ranch, but it's going to be burned to a crisp." She shook her head.

"Cry all you want," he whispered. "You've lost

your home. That's big." He tightened his arm around her, turning her to him and slipping his other arm around her for now, concentrating on consoling her.

But no matter how hard he tried to focus on those things, he couldn't fight the awareness of her in his arms. She was soft, sweet-smelling, with lush curves. He liked holding her far too much. He didn't want to look into her big, green eyes or at those rosy, full lips that were visible now. Again, he almost groaned aloud thinking about her.

He was taking her home with him. He'd already had her in his arms twice. That stunned him, because until today, they'd rarely acknowledged the other one's existence. He didn't know what she did or what she liked—he had never given two seconds worth of thoughts about her and he rarely had even seen her. This was all a first in his life—and not a welcome first.

He didn't want to like holding her in his arms. He didn't like wanting to kiss her, and he didn't want to find her desirable.

Claire Blake was as off-limits as if she was poison to his system. So why was he holding her close? Why was he so aware of her?

He should let her go. He should get her out of his arms, out of his pickup and out of his life as fast as he could.

How could he do that now when he had invited

her to come stay at his place? What was he going to do with her as his houseguest for the next few days?

Worse, how could he get through the night when all he wanted to do was kiss her?

Three

Her ranch burned. Her family home destroyed. Heirlooms passed down from generations gone. Treasured family pictures reduced to ashes.

Claire thought of all that loss and cried quietly. No matter how she tried to get her mind off her losses and get control of her emotions, she couldn't. And then she became aware of Jake's arms around her, strong and reassuring. She was being held closely against his rock-hard chest, something solid in her suddenly battered life. She tightened her arms around him, for just a moment yielding to the heady feeling that all was not lost and there was hope, however imaginary, that she was held tightly in the secure arms of a friend.

From the hour he was born, Jake Reed had been an enemy, just as she and all her family were his enemies. That feud had been drilled into her from the time she could toddle. As far back as she could remember in her childhood, she had heard how his family had rustled her family's cattle, stolen their horses, tried to claim water rights in the area where the ranch boundaries met. She'd heard how early relatives had fought duels with his family members, waylaid them and attacked them, robbing them, how they had set fire to their land and their houses.

She had no idea how much was truth and how much was exaggeration fueled by anger and hatred, but she had been taught to dislike all Reeds—and that included him.

For this moment, though, she could overlook the feud and the animosity to rely on the friendship and comfort he was giving her. He had saved her life and the dog's and the pups' lives, as well. For that, she would be eternally grateful to him. For the moment, she couldn't think of Jake as the enemy. Actually, far from it. Jake's arms felt wonderful around her, and when she had looked into his eyes, she had wanted him to hold her. In truth, she had wanted him to kiss her. That thought shocked her because kisses could only mean all kinds of complications in both their lives. There was another reason she didn't want to be attracted to him. Jake had a reputation of loving and leaving the ladies. He'd had more than his share of female friends in his life, and he always was the one to break things off as far as she knew.

Between the feud and his reputation, she didn't want to risk her heart with him at all.

Besides, they could never date. One date would bring out the animosity in both families. No, they had to remain adversaries.

She thought of their relationship thus far. The court battles they'd had. She recalled fighting him when he tried to divert two of the biggest creeks that provided them both with water. She had won in both cases, but then he had won a court battle over old boundary lines that gave him access to another creek that crossed her ranch.

Unfortunately, at present, his arms around her were the best feeling in the world. She knew she shouldn't enjoy being held so much, yet at a time when she felt incredibly alone in the world, his embrace and reassurances were solace for her broken heart over the loss of her home. She'd never get that kindness from her brothers or her father, and her friends were scattered in Dallas and she didn't keep up with them closely. She was close to some of the people who worked for her, but not close enough, since she was still their boss.

Right now, she relished Jake's arms around her. He was sexy, handsome, broad-shouldered, exciting.

He had saved her and the dogs—a man of action, able to get the job done quickly and efficiently—something her father and brothers had never done. She admired a man who could.

"Better?" he asked in a deep voice, and she looked into his dark brown, thickly lashed eyes that took her breath and held her immobile. She couldn't look away and her heart drummed, and she wanted his kiss—which was total insanity, because it would only muddle their lives. Up until the past moments, she would have been certain he would never want to kiss her, but she couldn't think that now. Not when she met his gaze.

The moment she looked into his sexy dark eyes, she knew he wanted to kiss her as much as she wanted him to do so.

She groaned. "We shouldn't ever," she whispered, and curiosity filled his eyes.

"We shouldn't ever what?" he asked in a husky voice. "Kiss? We both want to. We're adults, both single. Why not?" he added, and she was lost. The slight dark stubble on his jaw and chin added to his ruggedly handsome appearance. She felt as if his dark eyes could look right through her and that he knew every thought in her head.

She knew better, but his gaze was riveting and hot, stirring desire, something she didn't feel for any of the local cowboys or ranchers or any other man she knew. Until now.

She felt caught and held by Jake's gaze, and she also felt he could see the longing that was consuming her. Her desire was unwanted and unreasonable because they were deepest enemies, but she was ensnared and could barely get her breath. How long had it been since she had kissed a man or been kissed? How long since she had even been out with one?

Too long, she answered herself.

And right now, wanting to kiss him was all she could feel or think.

As his arm around her tightened, he leaned down the last few inches until his mouth covered hers. Excitement streaked through her, stirred by his mouth on hers, his tongue over hers. Feelings bombarded her, hunger for so much more of him, for his hands on her. She tightened her arms around him and kissed him in return, her tongue stroking his, hot, wet, so sexy. Desire shook her, and she held him tightly.

His kiss rocked her, building a raging response deep in her and making her want him more than she would have dreamed possible. She knew for certain that she had never been consumed by kisses that fanned the flames of longing the way his were. Even as her need intensified, she reminded herself that this was not the man to get deeply involved with. She shouldn't be melting in his arms.

He shifted slightly so he held her pressed closer against him with his arms still tightly around her. When she leaned away a fraction, his dark-eyed gaze consumed her. Yearning for more of him swept over her, as they kissed again.

Time ceased to exist for her, and she didn't know how long they kissed, but she finally realized that she had to stop kissing him as if they were the last two people on earth with only hours to survive.

With an effort, she shifted slightly and leaned away. Gasping for breath, she scooted out of his embrace, and he let her go. She couldn't tell from his expression what was going through his thoughts. She fought a battle with herself to avoid reaching for him again. How could she feel as if his kisses were the kisses of a lifetime when he was the one man on earth who was a total enemy? Only he wasn't an enemy at the moment. Right now, she just wanted to hold tightly to him and be kissed by him again and forget what she was losing.

Instead, she moved back, staring at him as if she had never seen him before in her life. She almost felt that way. She shook her head. "How do we—I mean, do we go back to the way we were and have always been—feuding neighbors?"

"Think what you will," he said in a husky voice. "You can go right back to the same feelings about me, but there is absolutely no way I'm ever going to forget or regret kissing you."

Her heart thudded again. "Maybe there's no going back to the way it was, but we have to move on from this."

"Yeah. I agree there's no going back to the way things were. We've crossed that line. Our relationship just changed forever," he added.

She shook her head. "I don't think our relationship really can change. That old feud is too much a part of each of our lives. We've lived with it since we were toddlers."

He raised an eyebrow and looked slightly amused. "I will never again see you the same way as I did before we kissed," he repeated quietly in a voice that was as intimate as a caress. All the time he talked, he stared intently at her as if he had never seen her before in his life.

She felt her cheeks flush with heat. "You can't turn off a century-old feud like tap water."

"We just made a good start on it." He slipped his forefinger beneath her chin to tilt her face up so she would look at him. "I'm willing to try. Are you?"

Her pulse jumped again as she gazed into his dark eyes and thought about their kiss. "Oh yes. I'll try," she answered, and it came out a whisper. She felt she had to move away from him, or she would be in his embrace and they would kiss again. While half of her wanted that, the other half warned she would regret kissing him. There was no way they could shake their past, their mistrust—actually, their dislike for each other. You couldn't turn off a lifetime of feelings in a morning. You couldn't really ever turn it off. Not when it had been part of their lives always. Deepest enemies.

This little flare of attraction wouldn't last. She had taken Jake to court before and won against him. She had lost to him, too. But the battle was always there, and she didn't think kisses would change everything between them. As fast as she thought that came another thought—his kisses were like no others she'd ever had in her life.

He wasn't going to be easy to get over. His kisses might be impossible to forget.

She looked up into dark brown eyes that hid what he was thinking. How little she actually knew about him. Could she really trust him?

Her gaze lowered to his mouth, and her pulse jumped. At this moment she didn't care about their future relationship. She just wanted his mouth on hers again and his hands on her to make her forget her losses and the fire.

She caught her breath, blinking, trying to gather her wits. She scooted away, and he shifted back, more into the driver's seat. He turned and started the pickup and then glanced at her again. "Ready to move on?"

"Yes, thanks," she said, meaning it. He had salved some of her heartbreak of permanent loss. She was more composed. At the same time, she realized she had some new problems. Jake Reed had given her the best kiss of her life, but he was also a lifelong enemy of her and her family. How badly had she just complicated her life?

Jake concentrated on his driving. Claire was as quiet as he was, and he suspected she might be in just about as much shock. She had the fire, the loss of her house, her scorched and burned land to worry about. She also had their kisses to think about.

She had just turned his life topsy-turvy. It was an understatement to tell her that he would never forget their kisses. He couldn't stop thinking about them.

They were fleeing a raging inferno behind them, and he was fighting a raging internal fire that made him want to pull off the road, take her into his arms and kiss her for hours.

He had never reacted this intensely to a woman he barely knew and hadn't even been attracted to in the past. He turned the pickup and finally got back on one of his ranch roads, a dirt track that was little more than two ruts with weeds growing up the center, but he knew where he was—it would lead back to a better road and eventually to his cabin.

And she was coming home to live with him for the next few days. Or weeks. He almost groaned over that thought. He hadn't been able to resist kissing her today. How was he going to resist kissing her when he took her home with him? Common sense said he should resist. They had been enemies all their lives, and now was not the time to get deeply and intimately involved with her. Because of her losses, she was emotionally vulnerable, and he didn't want to hurt her.

She could tangle up his life in a huge way. Right now, he was already tied in knots, confused by the hunger for her, hot, intense and constant—and by his need to get a grip on himself and get back to the way he had always viewed her.

Too late for that. The barn door had been opened, and the horses had already left. A few kisses and she had already complicated the hell out of his life.

So why couldn't he stop thinking about kissing her again?

He could think of too many reasons why he shouldn't—they were lifelong enemies. For years they had fought each other over ranch problems. They didn't even like each other. No, he had to amend that one. They didn't know each other, really. All he had were preconceived notions about her. And she definitely didn't know him. The last reason was a doozy: their families would be enraged if they even became friends.

"You're very quiet," she said softly, and he glanced briefly at her to see her looking intently at him. His gaze lowered as he looked at her lips, and he thought about their kisses.

"Just driving," he answered, focusing on the road and taking a deep breath.

"If you're having second thoughts about taking

me home with you, I'll try to keep out of your way, and tomorrow maybe you can take me to town, and I can find a place to stay."

He glanced at her again and felt a twinge of guilt for thinking she would be a problem houseguest. He smiled at her before turning his attention back to his driving.

"I'm fine about taking you home with me. You need a place to stay, and my cabin is roomy enough that we won't be in each other's way. Stop worrying. I wouldn't have asked you if I hadn't meant it," he said, thinking the real problem was keeping his hands off her.

Her kisses had set him on fire, and he wasn't going to forget them for a long time. He took a deep breath and tried to think about the fire, his cabin, his employees and his livestock—everything and anything besides Claire. How could she possibly be that sexy?

He forced himself to stare at the dry ruts and weeds until he got hold of himself. Then he allowed himself a glance at her, just a quick look. She was staring ahead, her emotions evidently under control.

She turned to look at him, and for an instant their gazes met. He felt the jolt all the way to his toes, and that's when he began to worry if he'd ever get hold of himself again. The urge to pull over, take her into his arms and kiss her again was as strong as ever.

He had to get out and spend some time with one

of his sexiest, best-looking, most fun women friends. He had some who would fit that description. And not one of them had ever set him on fire with her kisses the way his feuding neighbor had today. Thinking about it, he shook his head.

"Is something wrong?" she asked in a soft voice.

"I was just thinking about my livestock and the fire," he lied. He wasn't about to tell her what he was really thinking. "The guys saved the animals, and that's an enormous relief. I guess you feel the same about yours."

"Oh my, yes. Thank heavens they got mine moved. That's something I can think about that's very, very good."

He smiled at her again, glad she sounded in control of her emotions and positive about her livestock. She didn't sound bothered or in a dither, but then, he hoped, neither did he sound that way. He just *felt* that way. If he could forget her kisses, his life and his thoughts would calm and settle into his usual routines.

Unfortunately, he had a suspicion he wouldn't forget them in a lifetime.

He drove in silence, and she was quiet, seeming to be lost in her thoughts, so maybe she was adjusting to the situation.

In a short time, he turned up the cleared drive to his cabin. "There it is," he said. What he called his cabin anyone else would call a mansion, even if it was in the woods. The sprawling two-story river home was big and roomy, made of logs with an enclosed wraparound porch. Behind it ran a wide, rippling creek with cottonwoods scattered along the banks. To one side in the front was a man-made waterfall and a pond with exotic plants along one bank and tubs of blooming multicolored water lilies. There were beds of exotic plants and flowers next to the porch of his cabin. There were lifelike statues of wildlife—a mountain lion in a tree, a couple of grazing goats, a collie. He followed a wide drive around the cabin to a six-car garage. The drive was bordered by more green plants and flowers. A statue of a man fishing was at the creek's edge.

She laughed. "So, this is your fishing cabin in the woods, huh? I don't believe we're going to exactly rough it out here."

He smiled at her, his heart jumping as her eyes sparkled with laughter.

"I figured I might as well have something I like," he said.

"It's a fine place, and so pretty on the creek," she exclaimed. "A wonderful home."

"Thanks. I enjoy it out here."

As he parked on the drive near his back door, he turned to her. "I'll put the dog and her pups on the enclosed back porch. What's her name?"

"I don't know, actually. I called her Queenie. I've

never seen her before. I just happened on to her having her pups today."

"No kidding?" he exclaimed, glad she'd stopped to help the dog and pups, because if she hadn't, most likely they would have perished in the fire. "That's great," he said and was rewarded with another smile that made his pulse jump and made him think about kissing her again.

"The fire may have driven her from her home. I don't recall seeing her before. She doesn't have a tag. For a while there, I thought she was yours."

"If she doesn't have a tag, then I have the right people here for her—my neighbors the Andersons."

"I know the Andersons."

"Charley Anderson has three teenage daughters. The girls love dogs and cats. Any time we have animals wander onto the ranch, I call them. They come get them and they either reunite them with their owner or give them a home—with them or with friends. Are you willing for me to turn Queenie and her pups over to them?"

"Yes. It sounds like a good deal for all concerned, especially Queenie."

He took out of his phone and began typing. "I'll text them right now, and Queenie and her pups will soon be on their way back to their owner or to a good home."

"Great," she said. "That's a big relief." When he was done, he walked around the truck to climb into the back. She followed him to the side of the bed, and he picked up two puppies to hand to her.

"You take these, and I'll carry her and the other pups to the porch for now until the girls come," Jake said.

They had just settled the dogs and the pups when his phone buzzed with an incoming text. He looked at it. "The girls will be over soon to get Queenie and her pups." He sent an answer and looked up, smiling at Claire. "They'll be good to these pups, don't you worry."

"Thanks again. I'm sure it'll all work out."

As they walked to the door, he wanted to take her arm, to touch her again. But if he touched her again, there was a chance he might kiss her again, and that was something he had to resist. Something he had to stop thinking about.

What was it about her that had him constantly wanting her, constantly aware of her? She wasn't doing one deliberate thing to cause his response. He needed to remember who she was. Remember that Reeds and Blakes didn't mix and keep his distance.

He didn't like her family, and she was part of them. Even if she wasn't one degree like her bully brothers, she was still related to them. They had the same bloodlines, same parents, same home life, and somewhere that had to come out.

And her family wouldn't like her going out with him at all. If he did go out with her, he knew he'd have to watch his back, because those two older brothers would jump him some night if he let his guard down.

Jake couldn't figure out why he was so attracted to her. He knew a lot of good-looking, fun women who didn't come with problems and dreadful relatives who hated him. Definitely no one else whose family had fought with his well into a second century.

Why did she take his breath away, make his heart pound and stir all sorts of longings? Even now he wanted to stop, take her into his arms and carry her into his bedroom and spend the rest of the day and night there with her.

That acknowledgment shocked him, and he stopped and turned to look at her. She noticed and paused, her brows arching as she got a quizzical look. "What? Food in my teeth? Ink on my face? You're staring at me as if there's something."

"There's something, all right." His voice was thick with desire.

She blinked and held her hand up, palm out as if motioning him to stop. "Never mind that I asked. I don't want to know."

"No, you don't, but I'll tell you anyway, because I'm puzzled. I don't understand why our kisses are so—" he paused and narrowed his eyes as he thought "—so intense, unforgettable…so damn sexy. We've barely spoken until today, and we don't even know each other."

"Oh, we know a lot of things we don't like about each other, but we know very little we do like—that's the part where we're strangers," she answered. A second passed before she added the dagger. "But all we need to know is that I'm a Blake and you're a Reed. So, I think we should forget our kisses and get on safe subjects and keep a little distance between us."

"You're right. Kiss forgotten," he lied. "We'll talk about safe subjects. Ahh, here come the girls," he said as a large pickup pulled up. A man and three teenage girls stepped out.

"This time I hear you have a mama and pups," a tall blond-haired man said, pushing back his hat and smiling at Jake. "Are the dogs fire victims?"

"We're glad to see you, Charley, and yes, we do have a mama and pups. The fire probably is why she wandered away from her home." He said hello to the girls. "I think all of you know my neighbor Claire Blake."

Claire spoke to them as they greeted her.

"We'll get the dogs and be on our way. The girls can't wait to have the little pups."

Claire stood back out of the way as the Andersons gathered the animals and the bedding. Jake followed them to the car, and she went with him.

In minutes they waved goodbye to the Andersons, and she turned to smile at Jake. "Thank you. I'm sure the Andersons will do right by the dogs. And Charley told me to notify him if I have strays on my ranch and he'd come get the dog and find it a home. That's just wonderful."

"They're really good about it, and they don't seem to get overloaded or want to stop," he answered. Jake turned to face her. "Right now, I want to volunteer to help fight the fire," he said, knowing he needed to get away from her and try to forget their kiss. "I'm sure they can use extra hands. That fire is a record breaker."

"I think I should volunteer to help, too. I can't get out there and fight the fire the way you can, but I'll bet there are some things I can do."

He studied her a moment as he nodded. "You're probably right. We'll head down to the firemen's temporary headquarters. Meanwhile, c'mon, I'll show you where you can stay," he said, and she turned to walk with him into the cabin. They went through a wide hall with a polished hardwood floor and paintings of Western landscapes in gold frames hung on the walls.

They entered a spacious room with another highly polished hardwood floor. The room held an enormous wide-screen television, a game table and groupings of chairs and sofas. Down another hall, she glimpsed a movie room and a large dining room with a fruitwood table that would easily seat over twenty people. She noticed the surroundings, but she couldn't stop her eyes from wandering to her host. He walked close beside her, and she was aware of his height, of their shoulders and arms brushing lightly with each step.

And then she thought about her loss, about not even owning a house any longer, of not having a home, and she hurt again.

"I'm sorry," she said, taking a deep breath. "Everything I see makes me think about my house. I'll get accustomed to dealing with the loss, but right now, it's too recent."

"I'm sorry about your house, but your reaction is understandable, and you don't need to apologize. You don't need to explain it to me, either." He stopped in front of open double doors. "I'm across and down the hall where that door is open. This suite will be yours. Let's go look. I'm sure the bed has clean linens."

She barely heard what he said, because she was still thinking about him being "across and down the hall," which was oh so incredibly close. He looked the type to sleep in the buff—and then she tried to drop that thought as if it were a burning cinder. She looked up at him while he talked, but all she could think about was how handsome he was, and then she was lost in memories of his kiss.

She forced herself to focus on what he was saying. "...and I have someone who cleans every two weeks when I'm away and then comes once a week when I'm here. I have a cook when I'm here for very long, and I have a garden crew."

"Do they all drive out from town?" she asked, barely aware of what she said to him, because she was too conscious of his broad shoulders, how close he stood and his riveting dark gaze that kept her pulse racing. Now they were under the same roof, just down the hall from each other for how many nights? How was she going to be able to resist him? They obviously had something between them, or they wouldn't have shared a kiss that she didn't think she would ever forget.

"Most everyone who works for me lives around here," he continued, and she tried to focus on what he was saying. "There are houses scattered nearby— actually in walking distance. You just don't see them because of trees and bushes."

"Don't go to any trouble because I'm here. I can get along rather easily. A roof and a bed will be sufficient."

He smiled and nodded. "I'll get us some sandwiches. We may be working all night. You know where the kitchen is. You can meet me there." He left her to go to his suite, and she stood a moment to watch him walk away. He had long legs encased in tight jeans that were faded with wear. When he passed out of her sight, she turned to enter her suite and get ready to go.

The moment she stepped into her suite, she shook

her head. It was furnished with antiques, which she loved, recognizing some very old and very fine pieces, or else excellent reproductions. Her bed was larger than king-size with a frilly white canopy and a white bedspread.

"Some cabin," she said, shaking her head. There was no way his two-story mansion in the woods could be called a cabin, except that was what he called it. It was too big and too elegant. And now she would be spending the night with him here...alone.

Jake let out his breath when he entered his suite. If he kept busy the whole time Claire was with him, he probably could get by without kissing her again. He knew he had to try. He thought about his brother who had married her sister and how their lives had never been the same since. They were cut off from their families, living far, far away and keeping their whereabouts secret.

He couldn't stop the response he had to Claire, but he knew he needed to resist her. "Yeah, right," he whispered as he passed through his big sitting room into the bedroom. The suite held a custom-made bed, a large desk across the room and beyond the desk a big TV screen. He stopped by a table and picked up a remote control, pushed a button and in minutes he began to get pictures of burned acres, of parts of his ranch, pictures still being taken by Hap Green and sent back to him showing the fire and the damage already done. Hap didn't fly into the smoky parts, but the fire had already destroyed large areas, and they could get some shots of it in the distance. Jake shook his head and put down the remote, leaving the pictures on.

He got ready to go. He was certain the firefighters could use his help some way, and probably the workers would be glad to have Claire's help.

He went into the bathroom to use the facilities, and when he came out, his eyes lit on the huge bed. Unbidden, images of Claire sprawled out on the sheets assailed him. His breath grew ragged as he imagined him joining here there, making love to her. The thought nearly sent him up in flames.

He groaned and raked his fingers through his hair. "Damn," he whispered. Claire in his bed. He shook his head. "With her family and yours," he said aloud to himself, "that's the way straight to trouble."

So why was it exactly what he wanted?

Four

In less than half an hour, Claire joined Jake in the kitchen to eat a sandwich before they left. To take her mind off the fire and her loss, he tried to talk about something else.

"Is there a guy in your life?" he asked once they were seated at the table. He was suddenly aware he knew nothing about her except the family feud.

She looked startled, then amused as she shook her head. "No, there isn't. I don't go out often. I think I may intimidate some men. And I think some just don't like me because I'm a rancher and run the place. That tends to make me a little set in my ways and bossy, maybe."

He shook his head. "I've spent time with you now, and you weren't either. You're adapting to a huge change in your life," he said. "And bossy? You'd be a lousy rancher if you weren't. Someone has to be in charge."

"I know, but some guys don't want to take out a bossy woman who can run a ranch."

He shrugged. "Wouldn't bother me, I'll bet. Go out with me next Saturday night and we can see how I deal with going out with a bossy woman," he said, shocked again at himself and his reactions to her, even more shocked that he'd asked her out without giving any thought to the consequences of his invitation. And he knew he wanted her to accept. After lecturing himself to keep his distance from her, he was trying to get more entangled than ever.

He barely knew her, but he wanted an evening with her. As fast as that thought came, common sense said he shouldn't want to spend one single evening with her. She was a Blake. The family feud was as strong as ever. She wasn't the woman to get involved with. But he wasn't listening to his own advice.

Her eyes widened in surprise, and then she laughed, a sound of mirth that made him smile and want his arms around her more than ever.

"You're joking, of course. We'd set the town on edge, and our relatives would explode with everything from dismay to anger to rage. I don't think there would be one happy person in my whole clan who would approve of us going out together. You might find yourself in the middle of a fight with my brothers. For that matter, I doubt if there is anyone in your family who would approve of us going out together. In fact, I know they wouldn't, and I don't even know them." She leaned in toward him. "Tell the truth now—they wouldn't approve, would they?"

He looked down into her big green eyes, looked at her rosebud mouth, remembered their kisses and forgot what she'd asked him. He wanted her.

"I've never met anyone like you," he whispered. She blinked, and then her eyes widened. She drew a deep breath, straightened up and stared wide-eyed at him a moment before her gaze lowered to his mouth.

His heart thudded, and he wondered whether she was going to kiss him.

She shook her head as if coming out of sleep and stood, picking up her plate with her half-eaten sandwich. She stepped away from him, leaving more space between them. She stared intently at him. "I don't know why the attraction, or whatever it is, happens between us," she whispered as if to herself, but he heard her. He had finished his sandwich and a glass of water, and he stood to face her.

"I don't know, either, but we might be really missing something if we let what we feel go by without acknowledging it and acting on it. My reaction to you is unique in my life. I'd wager my ranch that your reaction to me is unique in yours, too."

The words were there between them, and she nodded. "That doesn't make it good."

"I'm sure it's something that shouldn't be ignored," he said with amusement in his voice, and she smiled in return as she shook her head.

"Let's not rush into something. I suggest you rethink that invitation to go out Saturday night. Your brother and my sister married and vanished. They haven't been home since they married because my sister knows my dad and brothers. My brothers' feelings about that feud are really strong. You take me out, and you're a marked man. I'm not about to do something that would get you hurt badly."

"I can't believe that would happen, and I'm not scared of your brothers," he replied. "But I don't want to cause you trouble with your family, so at this point in our lives, we can resist a night out together." He was disappointed, yet he had a feeling she was right. "There's no need to stir up a hornets' nest of trouble with families. We don't have any strong emotional ties, and we can still walk away from each other without it hurting. We better leave well enough alone."

"That's common sense, and I agree."

"I'm not sure I agree with myself," he said, glancing at her mesmerizing green eyes and wanting to kiss her right now.

"Hang on to your decision, Jake. We don't need to go looking for trouble."

"Might be the most fun ever," he said, lowering his voice and drawling his words. She drew another deep breath and gave a shake of her head.

"Jake, we better go and stick to helping out and forget any future together unless it's just waving at each other across the fence." She rinsed her dish and placed it in the dishwasher.

"You're right. Meet you on the porch shortly."

She went outside and sat in one of the rockers to wait. When he stepped out to join her, she came to her feet.

"C'mon. I've called the volunteer center, and they need us. And yes, they'll be glad to have your help."

"I'm willing to do what I can," she said.

"Good," he said, looking up at the sky. "Because we never got the rain they predicted, and now they don't think we will."

When he turned on the highway and headed toward the fire, she groaned. "It looks as if all of this part of Texas is on fire," she said, looking across the horizon. "This fire will get a lot of homes, barns and outbuildings. I just hope ranchers got their livestock and themselves out," she said, stunned by the smoke that totally hid every bit of sky and the dancing flames in the distance that spread as far along the horizon as she could see.

"They're going to need all the help they can get," he said.

"This has to be the worst fire in this area ever," she said softly, realizing a lot of people would lose everything. She fought back tears again, not only for herself, but for everyone who was being affected.

"Just try to focus on what you've saved. You have your animals. They didn't burn."

"Thanks to you, I didn't lose my life in this fire. It's just awful."

"Be careful tonight. Things happen, and everything can change in seconds."

"I'll be careful. I know what a close call I had today." She looked at his profile, her pulse beating faster as it did each time that she got on a personal level with him.

"We've always been enemies, but now..." She left the thought unspoken.

"Yeah," he said. "A kiss sort of changes things."

Unable to smile about it, she nodded. He was right. But his remark reminded her how temporary this truce was. It wouldn't last—it couldn't, with over 150 years of hatred in their backgrounds. They shouldn't kiss. The minute she reminded herself of that, her pulse jumped and beat at a faster pace. Jake's kisses were the sexiest she had ever experienced, and she had a feeling she was going to feel that way for a long time. She needed to try to forget kissing him, try to stop thinking about it, and above all, resist him from now on. Given their family history, kissing Jake was asking for pure trouble.

Her attention shifted as he drove to where temporary headquarters were set up for firemen. The area was filled with people. There were tents with hastily drawn signs for medical help, for tools, and a desk beneath a tree where volunteers could register to help. Another desk listed emergency help along with a posted list of missing people and other sources of information. She saw another tent with a hastily scribbled, crooked sign that stated Food.

"They almost have another town right here," she said as he parked his pickup in a row of vehicles.

"Well, I see where I need to go. I'll just look for you back here when I'm through." He turned to her. "You're in it now. If you want to quit, you'll have to wait until I'm back to take you to my place."

"Don't worry about me. I'm glad to help, and it looks as if they need it desperately. Let's go." She opened her door to step out.

"See you later," he called and was gone. She could see him moving through the crowd of people because he was taller than most. His broad shoulders made him look capable and reliable. She watched him until she lost sight of him, then lined up at the desk for volunteers. In minutes they had some people she was to drive to the hospital in Persimmon. To her surprise, Jake reappeared. He had a hard hat, a fire-retardant suit, goggles, gloves and a shovel.

"I'm digging ditches. They have some experienced firefighters flying in here, so they're getting more experienced help, which is good. When they let us go, I'll meet you back here. Take care," he said.

She worried about Jake, because the fire was formidable. Then she had to laugh at herself. Since when did she worry about a Reed? Instantly, an unwanted answer popped into her thoughts—since his first kiss. A kiss like no other in her life. A kiss that might be unforgettable. Also, since he saved her life.

Her family would be wild with anger if they knew she was with him. It wouldn't matter to them that he had saved her life. She hoped they didn't even find out about Jake. At least not for a long time. Her two older brothers would plot to beat him up and try to scare him into staying away from her forever. She knew their way of thinking. She hated their interference in her life, and she wanted them to back off. She would be furious if they did anything to Jake, but that would make them think she was really serious about Jake and they had something big between them. Caught between the proverbial rock and a hard place, she just hoped they didn't find out she had even talked to Jake.

Her dad would just be angry, but he wouldn't get involved now. He was getting feeble and wrapped up in his own world, plus he lived far away. To her relief, none of her brothers were in the area any longer, so hopefully they would never even know about Jake.

If she went out with him even just a few times, they would cut her out of the family and never speak to her again—they had been that way about her sister, although Regina didn't know their reactions, because she hadn't ever stayed around for them to snub her.

Her paternal grandparents and her dad had taken Regina out of their wills, ceased trying to communicate with her and told the family to never mention her name in their presence again, that she was no longer a relative as far as they were concerned. She had married a Reed, and to them, she had become a Reed.

Claire felt that the biggest loss was theirs, not Regina's. Sometimes she still hurt when she thought about her sister. Claire had looked up to her and loved her, and she had had so much fun with her when they were young.

She had despised the Reeds for taking her sister from her, blaming all Reeds for the calamity, but over the years she'd gradually begun to process it. Until today. Being with Jake had brought that resentment back. She wondered how bitter he was toward Regina for taking his older brother away from him. She thought about the pain and bitterness she'd felt when her sister had left, and now with Jake, memories were pouring back. They still hurt.

Suddenly she was too busy with the problems at hand and helping people to think about the family feud. She spent the next hours working furiously to help people with whatever they needed.

She worked with other volunteers, finding rides

for people displaced from their homes and lining up places for them to stay. With a furnished car, she took several people back to Persimmon to the hospital.

Time passed swiftly, and then as they moved through the night and into the early morning hours, the stream of people thinned to almost none. Someone thanked her for her help and told her to go home; they would call her if they needed her again.

She turned to find somewhere to wait for Jake when she saw him striding toward her.

He had a purposeful walk that drew her attention. The stubble on his jaw was thick, his black hair was tousled and he had streaks of dirt on his clothes. At the sight of him, her pulse jumped—she was glad to see him. He stopped in front of her.

"Good morning. They're sending some of the volunteers home," he said, his voice firm despite how quietly he spoke. "How about you?"

"The same," she replied. "I was told to go, and they would call if I'm needed again."

"Good. Let's go. Last night more trained firefighters flew in here, and they finally have the fire under control and are beginning to douse it." He jerked his head slightly. "C'mon, we'll go back to my cabin."

"I won't argue with that one," she said, falling into step beside him and keenly aware of his height as he walked beside her.

"Are you tired?" he asked.

She nodded. "Exhausted, really. But I was ready to stay if they needed me."

At his pickup, he held open her door. She slid into the passenger seat and watched him as he walked around to the driver's side.

"I may sleep all day," Jake said. "If you're hungry, I know an all-night diner if you want to stop and get something."

"I need sleep more than I need food."

"So do I. We'll just drive straight to my cabin and crash then," he said. "Thanks for helping."

"I was glad to do something to help," she answered, too aware of him so close beside her. His disheveled appearance just added to his appeal, and his broad shoulders gave him a look of strength and being capable of getting things done.

Lost in thoughts about Jake, she was silent as he drove back to his cabin. Everything about him amazed her. They had barely spoken in all the years they had been neighbors. Barely spoken until yesterday. Now she responded as if they were longtime friends, which they definitely were not. She figured their time to be civil to each other was definitely limited and that he was being courteous because she had lost her home in the fire. And maybe because of their kiss. That thought stirred another sizzle in her, and she drew a deep breath.

At his house he walked down the hall with her, his boot heels scraping on his hardwood floor. At the door to her suite, he turned to her. "Let's go look, make sure you have everything you need."

She gazed up into his brown eyes. He still had tangled locks of black hair falling on his wide forehead. "I'm fine. I was here yesterday afternoon and I checked. I don't need anything. I'll sleep in one of your T-shirts you loaned me." She looked down at her sooty jeans. "I just want out of these clothes."

"Can I help you there?" he asked, startling her until she saw the twinkle in his eyes, and she laughed as she shook her head.

"I think I can manage all by myself this time," she couldn't resist adding, flirting a little. He was smiling, but when she said, "this time," something flickered in the depth of his eyes.

"I'll remember to ask again," he said, his voice changing and getting deeper with a slight rasp.

"I should resist," she said solemnly and meant it. She shouldn't even flirt with him. She definitely shouldn't kiss him.

"We're entitled to a little fun after the day we've had." He reached out to touch her shoulder, his fingers light as a feather. "Thanks again for helping today," he repeated. "A little help can make a big difference."

She drew a deep breath as she looked into his brown eyes that held unmistakable desire, and her heart drummed. Her pulse jumped because there was no mistaking the hunger in his gaze. He wanted to kiss her. Common sense reminded her that she should turn away right now, ignore the need she felt, resist the intense awareness of his hand on her shoulder, of how close he stood, as well as the consuming look in those midnight eyes holding her in his spell. He smelled like smoke and had smudges on his cheek and shirt, but she didn't care. She wanted his kiss with all her being. She stopped worrying about consequences or the ancient feud.

"Jake," she whispered without even thinking about what she was doing. His arm slipped around her waist and she placed her hand so lightly on his chest, barely touching him, yet conscious of the contact. He was warm, hard and muscular. Her heart raced. "You know we shouldn't," she whispered, yet she leaned slightly toward him. Her lips tingled as her gaze lowered to his mouth.

"Yeah, I know," he answered in a husky voice while at the same time his arm tightened around her and he drew her closer.

"I can't resist you," she whispered again. She tilted her face up, looking at his mouth and then back to his dark gaze. She was hot, tingly, wanting him with all her being.

"Come here," he said in a voice that was the same as a caress. He tightened his arm again to hold her closer as his other hand went behind her head. She had her palm spread on his chest and felt the rhythm of his heart. He was looking at her as if he wanted to devour her.

While her own heart pounded, her lips parted as she stood on tiptoe to turn her mouth up to his. Slipping her arm across his shoulders, she drew his head down to kiss him. The stubble on his jaw was rough and prickly, but she barely noticed. Her heart raced as his lips moved so lightly on hers, and she moaned softly.

She wrapped her arms around his strong body and clung tightly to him. His waist was narrow, his belly flat and hard.

Moaning softly, she thrust her tongue over his. She felt on fire with wanting his hands and mouth all over her. Right now, she was lost in another fabulous, stormy kiss that made her want to be in his arms for hours.

He shifted, running his hand down her back, pulling her tightly against him. She felt his thick erection press against her, and she shivered as he deepened the kiss, fueling her own blaze.

She clung to him, aware of his hand sliding down her back so slowly, slipping down over her bottom.

She tried to hang on to common sense, knowing that if she didn't stop him, they would be in his bed making love soon.

She moved slightly and pushed against him just a bit, but he raised his head to look at her.

Gasping for breath, she stepped back to put space

between them. "We can't," she whispered. "We have way too much bad history between us."

Her heart pounded because his dark eyes were filled with desire, his lips slightly red from kissing her. She longed for him, wanting his hands and mouth all over her, but she was still able to pull her wits together enough to know that if she wasn't careful, she would upset her solitary life and get hurt badly, maybe a hurt that would last a lifetime. Jake was unique, desirable. At the same time, there was no way to ignore the fact that he was at the center of the feud she had grown up living in daily.

"We better say good-night," she whispered, turning away from him before they kissed again.

Standing behind her, he leaned close, whispering in her ear, "Claire."

She stopped as his arm circled her waist and he drew her back against him, his hard erection pressing against her bottom while he showered wet kisses on her nape and moved to her ear to let his tongue follow its curve.

She longed to turn into his arms and kiss him again. At the same time, she knew she should move away and stop before she was naked in his arms in his bed.

His warm breath blew on her ear, lightly tickling her, so sensual and heightening her desire.

"Claire, I want you," he whispered, and she trembled, fighting an inner battle, wanting to turn to kiss him, knowing she should step into her suite and stop risking her heart.

"I can't," she whispered, finally slipping out of his arms. He let her go, and she didn't look back.

She closed the door to her suite, leaned against it and closed her eyes, remembering his kiss, his strong arms around her, his consideration and care for her. She was drawn to him, and she shouldn't be. Not in the slightest. Her entire family despised him and all his kin. She would get hurt, because if she fell in love with him, they could never have even a sliver of a future—not even casual dating. He, too, had plenty of relatives here who would give him a bad time and be dreadful to her. "We can't," she whispered, knowing he couldn't hear her. She stood there against the door until she heard his boots as he walked away down the hall.

She still felt warm all over, recalling his hands and mouth on her, his body against her and his erection clearly ready for love.

Would she get through the next few days without losing her heart to him? She couldn't answer her question.

She needed to go to town, get some clothes, find another place to live and tell Jake goodbye before it hurt too much to walk away from him.

Even though they were neighbors she had never really known him, barely had any kind of dealings with him except when they had taken each other to court to fight over a ranch problem.

All that had changed, and if they kept kissing, she would be deeply in love with him. He had been kind, considerate and incredibly sexy.

She knew, if she wanted, she could go to bed with Jake now. They could make love, and it might be the best sex of her life. She didn't attract men, didn't date, didn't party except on rare occasions with friends in Dallas. So why not have a fling with Jake? Have sex with him? She might not ever have that choice again.

Because the risk would be falling in love with him—a deep, forever kind of love that he would never return. Love was doomed between them unless they did what her sister and his brother had done. If they both fell in love and married, would she want the kind of life her sister had—being forever in exile from her family?

Did she really want to run that risk?

She shook her head and whispered, "No."

Both choices were not what she wanted. She didn't want Jake to break her heart. She wouldn't want to marry him and get cut off from the grandparents, whom she loved. There were some in her family she really hoped to reconnect with—her dad and her brothers. There were others she deeply loved. Claire shook her head. She didn't want that kind of outcast life. Also, she knew Jake wasn't a marrying man. He'd had plenty of women in his life, and they just passed on through and were gone.

She had to keep her distance from Jake because he could be a heartbreaker, but right now she needed his help and a place to stay near her property.

Showering, she felt relieved to wash away the smoke smell and get it out of her hair. She washed her undergarments, hanging them in the bathroom to dry. Her jeans and shirt were saturated with smoke, so she washed them, too. Then, she put on one of Jake's T-shirts that she would sleep in.

Too late she realized that was a mistake. Inhaling his scent, she imagined the white cotton was the gentle touch of his hands on her skin. Right then she knew that despite being exhausted, she'd never sleep tonight.

Surprisingly, the next time she opened her eyes, sunshine spilled through the window. Momentarily, she was disoriented, and then she remembered she was at Jake Reed's cabin. As she thought about her home that had burned, a familiar emptiness filled her over her loss. Memories of the past twenty-four hours swept over her, but memories of Jake's kisses were more vivid than all others except her burned home.

She couldn't keep him out of her thoughts. She recalled being in his arms, held against his chest with his mouth on hers. Just remembering his kiss made her warm and tingly. She had to stop thinking about him. With a rustle of covers, she sat up and swung her legs over the side of the bed.

All her clothes were dry except her jeans. She stared at them in consternation, because she had to wear them, and she didn't want to wear wet jeans.

She dressed in her bra and panties and Jake's biggest T-shirt, which came down to midthigh level and covered her more than a swimsuit would have. She slipped her feet into her sneakers and grabbed the damp jeans. Hopefully, Jake would be occupied with breakfast, out doing chores already or something away from this part of the house and she could get her jeans into the dryer without encountering him. It wouldn't take more than twenty minutes to finish drying them in a machine.

She opened her door quietly and looked up and down the hall. To her relief, it was empty, and she hurried to his laundry room, flung her jeans into the dryer and in minutes was back in her suite with the door closed. She let out her breath, glad she hadn't seen him. Now if she could just get her dry jeans back, she would be in good shape for the day.

Twenty minutes later, she had her hair in a fresh braid, and she looked down the hall. Again, the hall was clear, so she raced to the laundry room, grabbed her warm jeans from the dryer—and almost ran into Jake as he came out of his kitchen.

Five

"Hey," Jake said, catching her shoulder when they bumped. "Sorry, I didn't see—" He stopped talking as his gaze traveled to her feet and back to her face and she saw the change in him.

"I had to dry my jeans," she said, in a breathless voice. "I washed all my clothes last night, and my jeans didn't dry. This was all I had to wear."

"Oh my," he said. The way he said it and the way he looked at her made her forget her clothes. All she could think about were his hands on her, his warm body against hers and the fact that she wasn't fully dressed. Stepping back slightly, he looked at her. His gaze went over her again, slowly, making her think about his hands and mouth going where he looked now.

"With legs like you have, you shouldn't ever hide them," he said, his gaze lifting to meet hers. "I have never seen you in shorts on your ranch. I've never seen your legs before. Not like this."

"Well, no, you haven't," she said, barely aware what she was saying to him. "You haven't because neither one of us ever gets close to our mutual boundary if we can avoid it, and I don't wear shorts to work on the ranch. Rattlesnakes, for one thing. Cockleburs, weeds, sunburn, thorny bushes for others."

"You have the best-looking legs in Texas."

She had to laugh at that one, and it helped put her more at ease. "Thank you, kind sir. But you need to get your eyes checked. I have scars from my barrel-racing days. I don't think my legs are quite that spectacular, but right now I need to cover them with my jeans, so if you'll excuse me," she said, hoping to hurry past him. She took a step closer to pass him.

When he didn't move, she looked up and met his dark, hot gaze. She couldn't get her breath, and her heart pounded. Desire filled his brown eyes. She had never before in her life felt as wanted by a man as she did right now with Jake.

When his gaze lowered to her mouth, her pulse jumped.

"Claire," he said softly, his voice coaxing and

filled with so much obvious longing that the tension she felt heightened.

"I need to go," she whispered, more to herself than him. "Jake, we've got to stop this. We don't have a future. We can't even have a lunch date. We can't go out together, and kisses just add to the problem."

"I don't think so," he said, sounding as if he meant it.

She shook her head. "Don't look at me like that."

She took a couple of steps to the side, and he placed his fingers lightly on her arm, barely touching her. "Wait a minute," he whispered.

As she paused, she drew a deep breath. She was only inches from him, starting to pass him, and he had barely touched her, but she stopped in her tracks and his voice played over her like a caress.

"Jake, don't hold me," she whispered. "You know I can't resist you."

"I'm not holding you," he answered, slipping his arm around her waist lightly. "You're free to walk away and you know it. Admit it, Claire. You want to kiss as much as I do."

"I might want to, but I know we shouldn't. I can't stop thinking about my brothers. I don't want you hurt by them." She didn't add that she didn't want a broken heart. He had left some of those behind. She knew that much about his past, and she didn't want that pain in her life.

"I'm definitely not afraid of your brothers, and

they won't hurt me, I promise you. They're not in town anyway and don't know what the hell is going on here."

"We can't kiss. I'm not even dressed."

"You think I don't know that? And I've never heard that for a reason to avoid kissing," he said with amusement in his voice as he leaned in to place light kisses on her throat. "You're gorgeous, Claire," he whispered, and all the amusement was gone from his voice. His earnest compliment drew her closer, and his wet kisses on her neck made her tremble. She ran her fingers into his hair, and when he looked up at her, she found his eyes hooded with an undeniable desire. A desire she knew was reflected in her own gaze.

"This is so foolish. I'm vulnerable and you'll break my heart," she whispered as his head dipped down and his lips continued their foray on her throat. She didn't know to whom she was saying those words—him or herself. "You're the real danger. Not my brothers. My heart is at risk."

He ran one hand so lightly on her nape, caressing her and arousing her, making her long for more. She moaned as an inner battle raged between what she wanted to do and what she knew she should do.

She should walk away from him. She was going to get hurt emotionally because if they kept touching and kissing, she would be in his arms, in his bed, and, worse, she would fall in love with him.

She couldn't afford that. He would never love her in return, and even if he did, they could never, ever have a future.

She didn't want an affair with Jake, and it would never be more than an affair, because he was not a marrying man. He'd never even kept his series of women in his life for long. They were seen with him for months, and then they were gone.

Even as she argued with herself, she thought about his kisses, to-die-for kisses that set her heart pounding, that made her want hours of sex and his hands and his mouth all over her.

Could she stand being one of the many women whose hearts he had broken in this little corner of Texas?

She knew the answer and knew she should walk away right now, but then he slipped his hand so lightly beneath the too-big T-shirt, his hand caressing her bare back and leaving a trail of fire that nearly consumed her.

His hand slipped around her waist, drifting up beneath the big T-shirt, pushing away her bra and then cupping her breast. She sighed with pleasure as his thumb stroked her nipple, and for a moment she gave herself over to his loving. She was vulnerable, lonely, hurt by the loss of her house, and Jake was stirring all the longings she tried to suppress, the craving for a strong man to hold her, to make love to her. And she could never find one better than Jake.

"You're gorgeous," he whispered. He cupped both breasts in his hands, toying with her, making her want more of him.

That nagging inner voice wouldn't be denied, however. Its warning echoed in her head until she wriggled away and stepped back, looking up at him and shaking her head. "We can't do this. I'll get hurt."

"I don't ever want to hurt you, Claire. And believe me, you're not going to fall in love with me because we kissed a few times," he whispered, his tongue tracing the curve of her ear.

"Ah, Jake, you know I want you," she whispered. They looked into each other's eyes, and she could no longer refuse him. She wanted his kiss. And he was right—surely she could kiss him once, twice more without falling in love and breaking her heart. She stood on tiptoe, pulled his head down and placed her mouth on his. Her tongue touched his, and then she was lost in his kiss as he wrapped his arm tightly around her, holding her pressed against him with one arm.

His other hand slipped down her back and then inside her lacy panties, over her bare bottom. She heard him inhale deeply, and then he slipped the panties off her hips, letting them fall to the floor around her ankles. While he kissed her, his tongue stroking her, building desire, he caught the hem of the T-shirt and drew it over her head to toss it aside. He stepped back to cup her breasts again and to look at her.

"You're absolutely beautiful," he said in a gravelly, raspy voice. His thumbs played so lightly over her nipples.

Lost in waves that rocked her, she clung to him with her eyes closed as need built from his hands so lightly on her breasts. She realized soon there would be no going back.

You'll get hurt.

That inner warning wouldn't be silenced, no matter how much she wanted to ignore it. Finally, she pushed against him and opened her eyes. The hungry look in his eyes made her tremble, but she kept her resolve. "Jake, I'm sorry, but I'm not ready for this."

Yanking up her clothes, she stepped out of his embrace, trying to avoid looking into his dark eyes that enticed her and melted her resistance.

She realized he wasn't arguing with her or trying to stop her, and she was glad because she knew she couldn't stand one more minute of his seduction. Gathering her things as fast as she could, she wrapped the big T-shirt around her and walked away from him without looking back.

Dressed and ready for the day, she still couldn't get him out of her mind. Jake—a Reed.

There was no denying she wanted his loving, his kisses, his hands all over her, his male body against hers. With him, she knew she'd have the best sex of her life. But how could she make love to him, fall for him and forget him, when she'd never be able to really get away from him?

He had a big ranch next door to hers—they were both permanently tied to the sprawling Texas land they owned. One day she would have to live next door to him and watch him marry someone else.

She went over it all again in her mind and knew what she had to do. She had to fight the temptation. She had to get out of his cabin and off his property.

"Jake, there's no place for you in my life," she whispered as she walked out of her borrowed room to find him for a ride to Persimmon. She had to go to town and get some clothes.

She found him in the kitchen. The second she walked in, he turned around to her. His gaze swept over her, and she felt her pulse jump.

Jake crossed the room, approaching her, and with every step nearer, her heartbeat quickened. He had the sleeves rolled up on his blue denim shirt that was tucked into tight faded jeans—working jeans. He had on boots, and it took her breath away to look at him.

And then he was only a few feet away, standing close, smiling at her, his hungry gaze on her, and all the determination she'd felt when she'd made the trek from her suite seemed to buckle. In its place came one question: People survived broken hearts, didn't they?

* * *

Jake's gaze slid over her, and he drew a deep breath. In tight jeans, a red T-shirt and boots, she looked fantastic. "You look great in those clothes, but I can understand wanting a change. I'll take you to town," he said. His voice deepened and became huskier in reaction to looking at her. Since when did he find his neighbor sexy, appealing and absolutely fascinating? He knew exactly when—since that fabulous, to-die-for kiss that he didn't think he would ever forget. And each one after that first kiss had been just as overwhelming and stunning.

"Jake, on the way into Persimmon to get clothes, I'd like to go look at my house. There might be some things in fireproof boxes that made it through the fire. I'd like to go see. There are a couple of boxes I had money in."

"I hope not a lot of money."

"No."

"Ever hear of a bank?"

She gave him a look, and he noticed the moment when she realized he was teasing her.

"Ever hear of minding your own business?" she replied, and he laughed.

"Let's get breakfast and then we'll go," he said. "I've got sliced strawberries and blueberries. I can scramble eggs and we can have toast," he said, but his thoughts weren't on breakfast as she walked closer. He couldn't stop thinking about how much he wanted to make love to Claire. How could her kiss totally change his feelings for her?

It took all his willpower to concentrate on getting breakfast on the table and keep his hands to himself.

She helped him, putting plates on the table, filling cups of coffee and orange juice. When they were ready, he held out her chair, his hands brushing her so slightly, yet he was aware of the contact.

As they ate, she was quiet, but he couldn't miss the glances she'd flick in his direction when she no doubt thought he wasn't looking. The look in her eyes was not that of someone who viewed him as an enemy. The look in her eyes made him want to drop everything, take her into his arms and kiss her. He ate his breakfast, noticed that she didn't eat much of hers, and then he stopped her from trying to clean the kitchen.

"Betsy comes today to clean, so leave the dishes. Let's head out to your ranch and then go to Persimmon so you can buy some duds."

"That will be a welcome relief," she said. "I dread seeing my house, but there were some metal containers that had important things, so I want to see how they fared and maybe pick them up."

"They could be too hot to move yet. I can get some guys to go get them if I can't get them into the pickup. We'll see," he said, doubtful she had anything that made it through the fire. "It may still be smoldering, and we need to be careful because some areas are probably still burning and can just flare right back up."

"I'll make it quick. I don't think it'll take long to look."

He nodded, looking at her thick braid and wondering how she would look with her hair loose. He realized he was lost in thoughts about running his hands through the thick red hair, seeing it splayed against his pillow, and he turned away, shooing her out of the kitchen. He had a feeling if he didn't, they might not get to town this morning.

They drove across land that still smoldered, and occasionally they passed a small fire, flames still flaring where there was something left to burn. Some structures were either completely gone or were partially burned and still standing but looking ready to collapse.

"Damn, it looks like a war zone. Are you sure you want to keep going?"

"Yes, please. I had two boxes I used for safes. I want to get those. There's money and papers I need."

"Okay. Make this fast. Fires are unpredictable."

"I'll hurry," she answered and lapsed back into silence. He knew she was hurting and this drive to her ranch wasn't going to do her any good that he could see, but if she could salvage something, he would help. He glanced at his watch, because they weren't going to stay long. He'd bring her back if necessary, but he didn't like being here and felt certain they shouldn't be breathing the fumes.

When they entered her ranch, the damage was extensive. Her barn, outbuildings, employees' houses—all were in smoldering ruins. And then her house came into view, and he heard her groan and he hurt for her. There was nothing left of her house except mounds of ashes, burned wood that looked as if a breeze would crumble it. He knew how he would feel if it was his home.

He pulled close and got out of his pickup as she went ahead, handing her a bandanna that she put over her mouth. He had given her gloves and had a pair for himself, because he could glimpse little flares of flickering flames under the rubbish. They both wore boots. He hoped she would hurry, because it wasn't a good place to be.

"Do you want me to put the containers I find into my pickup?"

"If possible, yes. If it takes two to move something, just let me know."

He walked through the rubble. There were metal containers, some too big for her to handle, one that took both of them. She called him to another one.

"I need this one. This is the main one. It's got money and papers," she said, and he looked down at a large metal box with handles on both ends and a dent in the lid. Recognizing the box, he stared at it. "I'll be damned," he said without realizing he had spoken out loud.

"Turn this over," he told her, taking hold of one of the handles, because he knew it was heavy and would take both of them to turn and get it into his pickup. Anger washed over him as he bent to roll it over.

Jake looked at dents and scrapes across one part of the bottom. It was covered in ashes and burned black bits of wood. He swept his arm across it and brushed it off, peering at letters that someone had tried to scratch over while his heartbeat quickened, and his anger increased.

Just as he suspected. This big metal box had belonged to his dad.

Six

"What are you doing?" she asked. "This has money in it and some of my important papers. This is the main container. My dad kept papers in it and guns. He left it for me. I want to take it with us."

Anger made Jake hot, and he looked up at her. "This metal box used to belong to us. My dad's name is scratched in the bottom side. He kept money in it until it was stolen," he said, feeling a deep flash of anger, because her dad and brothers must have been the thieves who robbed his dad. Suddenly he was caught up once again in the feud with her family, remembering that his dad always claimed Claire's father and brothers had been behind the theft.

"This can't be yours," she said, a note of impatience in her voice. "This belonged to my dad. He had it before I went to college. He said it was my grandfather's."

"I think not," Jake said, trying to brush off more debris. "Someone has tried to scratch over a name. We'll take this and clean it up, but I know this box. The corner was dented like that when we had it because a couple of guys who worked for my dad dropped an anvil on it."

As Jake's anger intensified, he remembered times he'd fought with her brothers. He remembered the things her dad had done when her family owned the ranch. Fences cut, livestock stolen—her family was smart enough to never keep the livestock, but his father always thought her dad and brothers rustled cattle and sold them, moving them quickly so they wouldn't get caught.

He thought they did it to be ornery, not for the money at all.

"This is my family's box. Underneath all those scratches, I'll bet I find the name Reed," he said. "Help me lift it." She glared at him as she grabbed a handle and they hoisted it into his pickup.

"Let's get the rest of these metal containers," he said, hurrying through the debris and coughing from the fumes. Anger rocked him, and he could remember other incidents of vandalism that had happened years earlier to their ranch, things his dad had blamed on the Blakes. Jake needed to get himself away from Claire and remember the feud, because he might not be able to trust her any more than he trusted her dad or her brothers. She was a Blake just as much as the rest of her family. She might be far more like them than she admitted. He didn't want to get tangled up emotionally with some woman who had the same blood in her veins as her dad and those thugs that were her two older brothers.

Angry and grim, he worked in silence, gathering up three more containers. "Let's go. We'll come back for more, if need be. No one else is going to come get this stuff. Not out here. Let's get out of here and go where we can breathe fresh air. I promised to take you to Persimmon, but we're going back to the ranch first to wash this stuff off."

"I agree," she said, coughing and climbing into his pickup.

With both of them coughing, they rode without conversation, and once they were away from her place and all the smoke and debris, he took off the bandanna and tossed it into the back. She did the same. They remained silent all the way to his place. When he parked, he turned to her.

"Let's get that box out on the ground. I'm going to shower first, and then I'll clean it up and see if we can read the name that someone has tried to scrape away."

"All right," she said, glaring at him. He felt certain

the box had belonged to his family, and he hoped he could prove it. He wondered why she was insisting they hadn't stolen the box, unless she thought her family would never break the law and steal something.

He knew better, but he didn't want to tell her, because she might not know some of the nasty things they had done. She acted like she didn't know. If he learned she had ever helped them steal and do things to his family… His anger rose as he thought about that. He wondered just where she fit in and how much like them she was. Even if she didn't know all they had done, he didn't want to find her appealing. They had too much history between them. And he had a feeling the vandalism and the thefts had been directed only at his family because of the old feud. He had never heard anyone else complaining of vandalism or theft by any Blakes. The old anger that her dad and her older brothers could stir came back full force, and he remembered why he would get so angry at them. Far too often, they wiggled out of blame for anything they had done.

"We have to get out of these smelly clothes. I want to throw mine in your washing machine," she said. "I can't wear these to town or even in your house. I'm getting the hose to wash some of this off out here before I go inside. You may want to do the same."

"Good idea," he said. "I'll get the hose." He wanted to get washed up and then wash that box.

He was absolutely certain it would have the name Reed carved into it, and he couldn't wait to show her.

He turned on the hose, walking back to hand it to her first. "Go ahead. I'm taking off my shirt."

"I'm sure you won't mind if I do the same. I'll have as much on as I would if I were in my swimsuit, and I can't stand this smell any longer," she said, placing the hose in the flower bed. With her back turned, she yanked off her boots and socks and then pulled off her red T-shirt.

The moment she did, his mouth went dry, and he forgot the fire, the smoke, the smell, the metal box and everything else except looking at her. Her waist was tiny, her skin looked smooth and she looked soft and irresistible. She kept on the jeans and ran the hose over herself and then turned to hold the hose out to him. When she turned around, she still wore her jeans, but above her waist, she wore only her lacy white bra, which was wet and clinging. Her skimpy bra revealed lush curves that made him instantly aroused, wanting to reach for her.

She was breathtaking and incredibly sexy. She splashed water from the hose over her full breasts and he fought to keep from walking closer, taking her into his arms and kissing her senseless while he caressed those gorgeous breasts. As she ran the hose over herself, she had her eyes closed. "Oh, that is such a relief," she said softly to herself.

An intense urge swept him to close the slight distance between them and take her in his arms. He wanted to step close and remove her bra. He wanted to fill his hands with her full breasts that looked so soft.

"I'm sorry to go first," she said with her eyes still squeezed tightly closed while she held the hose above her head and let water shower over her.

He yanked off his shirt, tossing it aside as he walked to her, wrapped one arm around her narrow waist while he took the hose from her hand and ran it swiftly over himself and tossed it aside.

Startled, her eyes flew open. "Jake?" She looked up at him, and he saw her expression change.

"You're absolutely gorgeous," he said. He was already breathless. Eagerness made him shake, and he was rock hard.

She blinked. "I thought you were angry with me," she said.

He didn't answer but gazed into her big green eyes and saw the transformation in her expression as her lips parted and her gaze shifted to his mouth. Her hands rested on his chest, and she slipped one arm across his shoulders while she ran her other hand over him, tangling her fingers in his chest hair.

His heart pounded, and he could barely get his breath. He unfastened her bra and pushed it down so he could cup her breast in his hand. She gasped and closed her eyes while she leaned closer and tightened her arm around him.

She was so incredibly soft. Her full breast filled his hand. Her eyes fluttered open, and she looked at his mouth as she drew his head down. He placed his lips on hers, his tongue slowly stroking hers as he caressed her breast.

She moaned softly, moving her hips against him.

For minutes, eons, seconds—first it seemed long and then it seemed short—he kissed her and caressed her. She was wet, warm and bare. He wanted her with all his being. He was aroused, wanting her more than he could remember desiring any woman ever.

He wanted to be inside her, to make love to her and forget the consequences.

Suddenly she wiggled slightly, leaning away, and then she stepped out of his embrace and shook her head. "Jake, stop. We were at each other's throats only a few minutes ago, the family feud still alive and strong. I can't do this. You're a Reed. We're not going to tangle our lives and emotions," she said, stepping back, grabbing up her shirt and holding it in front of her as she raced away from him, unlocking the door with the key he had given her and disappearing inside the house.

"Dammit," he said quietly as he let her go. He ached with wanting her. He wanted to bury himself in her soft body, to have her fiery, bone-melting, unforgettable kisses.

He groaned as if he had a terrible wound. She was right. They had over a century of feuding between their families, and he suspected there would be plenty more fussing between Claire and him when he cleaned up that metal box, because he was absolutely certain it would have the Reed name cut into it.

Even as he made the decision to let her go and thought about the feud, their differences and the anger between them with more to come, he wanted her. He craved her, wanted her in his arms. He was ready to make love to her and couldn't keep images of her gorgeous body out of his thoughts. At the moment he didn't give a damn about the feud, the metal box, their differences or the future. He just wanted to make love with her.

He ached to caress her lush, soft, fantastic breasts. She was breathtaking, beautiful, the sexiest woman he had ever kissed. And she wasn't trying to be sexy. What if she wanted to be? That thought could send him up in flames, and he tried to shift his thinking.

"Damn," he muttered under his breath, clenching his fists. He had to ignore her, forget kissing her. "Impossible," he whispered to himself. He would never forget kissing her. He couldn't possibly forget the feel of her breasts in his hands.

She had him tied in knots. They had spent their lives disliking each other, fighting each other or ignoring each other until their first kiss—that sexy kiss like no other he had ever experienced.

He groaned, grabbed the hose and let it shower cold water over him, wishing he could wash away memories of her body, her mouth, her soft breasts, her kisses, but he knew that he would never forget them.

How he wished some woman would come along who could wipe her out of his memory.

Claire Blake. A Blake with a family of relatives who had fought his for over a century. He had to forget her.

He knew he never would. Not in this lifetime. Worse, he wondered if he would ever stop longing to kiss her.

Swearing quietly, he tossed down the hose, which hadn't really cooled him. He turned off the water, gathered his shirt and boots, and headed for the house. She had hooked the screen door, and he couldn't get in. He rang the bell and waited.

Finally, she came to the door, and he wanted to groan, to gnash his teeth, to ask her if this was a new form of torture that she was using because of the feud.

She had a towel wrapped around her head, hiding her hair, and another wrapped around her gorgeous body—a body that had to be very naked beneath that green towel that matched her eyes.

"Sorry, I didn't intend to lock you out of your house," she said, her cheeks turning pink as she gave him a long, intense stare and he wondered what she was thinking.

She was looking so gorgeous, so appealing, that he couldn't find his voice. What was wrong with him?

She must have picked up on his discomfort, because she suddenly looked self-conscious. "This wasn't such a good idea," she said. "I'll see you later. I need to get dressed." Then she turned to walk away, and he watched her go, that towel clinging damply to her bottom, her long, bare legs revealing that the lower part of her was as gorgeous and sexy as the upper part. Her legs were marvelous. Long, long legs that he would like to feel wrapped around him.

He groaned and closed his eyes to try to stop thinking about having sex with her. He opened his eyes quickly. He wanted to look at her as long as he had a chance. She would come back all covered in something that would completely hide her fabulous body.

He went to his suite, closing the door. From today on, he would never see Claire the way he had before. Every inch of his being wanted her in his cabin and in his arms again. In his bed.

He swore as he got ready to shower and walked into his big bathroom. It was an architectural gem, with a curved shower, huge sunken tub and a glass wall that afforded him an unobstructed view of the outside, though no one could see in. One wall held a built-in floor-to-ceiling tank of exotic tropical fish, while a floor-to-ceiling mirror comprised another wall. Right now, he saw only the shower. He walked into it and turned on the cold water. "Do your stuff," he said to the cold-water faucet. "I have to forget her. A Blake. I don't want to entangle my life with her. As if she would let me. Oh damn. How long will it take me to forget her when she lives on the neighboring ranch? And that is my family's box out there, and it was her thieving dad and brothers that stole it from my family."

Jake shook his head. He could never be friends with her, never trust her. He shouldn't ever kiss her again, not even touch her. He'd be polite, let her stay at his cabin because he had already issued the invitation, but she would soon move on, and when she did, he needed to go back to the way it always had been—not speaking to each other, never socializing, absolutely never kissing.

He groaned. Why was the woman whose family had spent lifetimes feuding with his the one with the hottest kisses he had ever known?

He shook his head. He had to avoid her. She might make that easy for him to do, because she'd be angry as a bear when he took that metal box away from her.

He felt another hot flash of anger over the stolen box. Her brothers had probably stolen it and given it to their dad, who'd kept it and everything in it. He thought about calling his father and telling him, but his dad was probably happily fishing and enjoying his retirement—there was no point in bringing up a bad subject that still didn't have a good solution.

Meanwhile, he needed to get himself away from Claire. They had no future together. So why couldn't he stop thinking of how she looked in that green towel? Damn. The cold water had done nothing to help him.

Claire dried her hair and stared at herself in the mirror, but she didn't see her reflection. She saw Jake's dark eyes on her, remembered his hands moving lightly over her, remembered his mouth on hers as he kissed her.

Her heartbeat raced. She shouldn't be staying at his cabin, shouldn't have undressed in front of him. But the fumes from the fires had permeated her clothing and took her breath. She thought if she still wore her bra, she would be as covered as she always was in a swimsuit.

It must have been a psychological thing, because he had changed the instant she had revealed her bra. For a moment there outside, she'd been caught up in memories of his hands caressing her and the hungry look in his eyes.

With a shake of her head, she tried to stop thinking about Jake. They didn't have a future. Their families had fought since before Texas was a state. And he had accused her family of stealing that big metal box that belonged to her dad. It was her family's box. It had survived the fire, and she wanted it. It was rightfully hers. Her brothers had done some bad things, she knew, but they wouldn't steal.

She felt anger, but it wasn't as strong as other feelings: hunger for his kisses, yearning for his arms around her, for his hands caressing her. Despite everything, she wanted to be in his arms again. She moaned softly, desiring him, knowing she shouldn't, that she had to forget him and banish these taunting memories once and for all. And she needed to move out of his cabin as soon as she could and put distance between them. She looked at her palatial surroundings, the big bedroom with an elegant canopied four-poster bed that she suspected was an antique, the antique mirror with an elegant carved frame. *Cabin* was not the right description for his home in the woods. It was a castle. But it was Jake's, and as much as she reveled in its beauty, she had to leave it.

She didn't think her brothers had stolen that box from him or his family. That would be breaking the law, and they didn't do that. It was just a big metal box, and there were probably millions that looked just like it. There were scratches on it, but no readable names. It would have been obvious if her brothers had stolen it. They would have bragged about it eventually.

She was angry that Jake had insisted from the first second he saw the box that it had belonged to his family.

She shouldn't have gotten so chummy with him.

She shouldn't even be staying with him, but she'd never made friends with neighboring ranchers and had nowhere else to go. Her friends were in Dallas, friends she had made growing up, friends of her family, neighbors she'd had in town.

She considered her employees friends, but with this fire, they had terrible problems, too. They needed her help probably more than she needed theirs.

She and Jake were part of feuding families, and that wasn't going to change. The metal box was just one issue. There would constantly be other issues, because they saw life in different ways, and they didn't like each other's relatives.

She knew she was vulnerable because of her isolated lifestyle. She didn't often go to Dallas, where she had friends and at least some social life, but on the ranch, she was alone, in charge, and that made a difference in her relations with everyone who worked for her. Particularly the guys.

And then came Jake. Never had kisses excited her the way his had…

But he definitely wasn't the man for her—a Reed, like the other Reeds.

She should get out of his house, go into Dallas to her condo and never look back. But how could she do that when she was needed at the ranch? Her home had been totally destroyed. She had called her insurance agent briefly, but he couldn't do anything

Get Up To 4 Free Books!

Dear Reader,

IT'S A FACT: if you answer 4 quick questions, we'll send you 4 FREE REWARDS from each series you try!

Try **Harlequin® Desire** books featuring the worlds of the American elite with juicy plot twists, delicious sensuality and intriguing scandal.

Try **Harlequin Presents®** Larger-Print books featuring the glamourous lives of royals and billionaires in a world of exotic locations, where passion knows no bounds.

Or **TRY BOTH!**

I'm not kidding you. As a leading publisher of women's fiction, we value your opinions... and your time. That's why we are prepared to reward you handsomely for completing our mini-survey. In fact, we have 4 Free Rewards for you, including 2 free books and 2 free gifts from each series you try!

Thank you for participating in our survey,

Pam Powers

To get your 4 FREE REWARDS:
Complete the survey below and return the insert today to receive up to 4 FREE BOOKS and FREE GIFTS guaranteed!

"4 for 4" MINI-SURVEY

1 Is reading one of your favorite hobbies?
☐ YES ☐ NO

2 Do you prefer to read instead of watch TV?
☐ YES ☐ NO

3 Do you read newspapers and magazines?
☐ YES ☐ NO

4 Do you enjoy trying new book series with FREE BOOKS?
☐ YES ☐ NO

Please send me my Free Rewards, consisting of **2 Free Books from each series I select** and **Free Mystery Gifts**. I understand that I am under no obligation to buy anything, as explained on the back of this card.
❏ **Harlequin Desire®** (225/326 HDL GQ3X)
❏ **Harlequin Presents® Larger-Print** (176/376 HDL GQ3X)
❏ **Try Both** (225/326 & 176/376 HDL GQ4A)

FIRST NAME   LAST NAME

ADDRESS

APT.#   CITY

STATE/PROV.   ZIP/POSTAL CODE

EMAIL ☐ Please check this box if you would like to receive newsletters and promotional emails from Harlequin Enterprises ULC and its affiliates. You can unsubscribe anytime.

HD/HP-520-MS20

while the area was still burning and off-limits. She'd called the sheriff, her employees, her builder—the list was long. She had to stay and, once the fire was totally out, work with people to get her land cleared and, eventually, her house rebuilt.

There were so many things to do, but dominating her thoughts were memories of being in Jake's arms, holding him and kissing him as if they shared the last kisses of their lives.

"No," she whispered, shaking her head. She wanted to shut off the memories, stop thinking about him and his kisses and his hands on her, incredibly gentle, sexy and breathtaking. She needed to move on with her life and get back to her routine, where Jake had no part in her day.

But right now, that wasn't going to happen.

At least not as long as she was living in his house, kissing him, spending time with him and getting to know him and getting more obligated to him. She was wearing one of his shirts right now. How was she going to get free of him when she needed to stay in the area, take care of her business and live at his house because she had none?

She shook her head again and raked her fingers through her hair. She had to get Jake out of her thoughts. She was sure when she was out of his house and away from him, she would be able to bank these memories of him. She had to, because he was consuming all her thoughts now.

She groaned, tossed her head to get her long red braid away from her face and tried to think about what she needed to do, getting out a list she had made and retrieving her phone. She went to a desk in her room, got a notebook and her phone, and called her insurance agent to talk to him again about her ranch house. As she waited, she glanced down at a picture on the desk. It was in an old-fashioned wooden frame with flowers and held an old black-and-white picture of a little boy. She picked it up and looked at it and recognized the tousled black hair—this must be one of Jake's childhood pictures. He'd been a cute little kid. She stared at it. "You're messing up my life," she said. "Don't kiss me again."

"I can't make that promise," came a familiar deep voice behind her.

Seven

"Good grief, don't sneak up on me," Claire exclaimed, feeling her cheeks flush with embarrassment at him overhearing what she'd said about his kisses.

He looked amused with a faint smile as he came into the room. "I don't think I was too sneaky in my boots. They make a bit of noise on the wood floors," he said, and she could hear the laughter in his voice. She knew he was teasing, but he was annoying her again, and her embarrassment deepened.

"Well, I didn't hear you, and I wish you hadn't heard me."

He kept walking toward her, and her pulse beat

faster as he came within inches and tilted her chin up with his finger. She felt opposing reactions— she was annoyed that he was laughing, but she was turned on by his nearness. He was inches away, and that made her heart race and made her want him to lean close and kiss her even though she shouldn't. She was accustomed to controlling a lot of things and the people in her life. She couldn't do anything about the weather and fires, but people she could usually manage. But she couldn't manage Jake. He didn't work for her. He was independent, doing what he wanted to do, and he was a wild card in her life. She didn't know what he would do next. And she was far too drawn to him physically when she should avoid him, because they were still and forever would be feuding neighbors. How had she thought they could be friends? They were steeped in their family feud that would never change.

"You know, if looks could kill, I'd be stretched out on the floor," he said, and she heard the laughter in his voice that just made her more embarrassed and more angry.

"I think we need a lot more distance between us," she said, but the words came out breathlessly and she was lost gazing into his dark eyes that made her heart beat even faster and her desire more obvious. She couldn't get her breath because she knew he was going to kiss her, and she knew she was going to kiss him in return when she shouldn't. She should resist and get a wall between them.

She couldn't stop the anger she felt toward him, but desire was there just as strong. She couldn't understand her own reactions to him. She had never felt this way about any other man before. And then she didn't care. She just wanted his kiss, and her gaze went to his mouth as his arm slipped around her waist and he drew her to her feet.

His lips brushed hers lightly. She moaned softly, winding her arm around his neck and leaning into him, feeling his strong body against her. His fantastic body. Her heart pounded as she kissed him in return. "I wasn't going to do this ever again," she whispered.

"Yeah, I know," he said as he brushed another light kiss on her lips and then her ear. "I wasn't going to do this again, either," he whispered in her ear, his warm breath tickling her, making her want his mouth on hers more than ever. "You want to kiss me as badly as I want to kiss you."

"You and I are bitter enemies, Jake," she said, knowing she meant those words as a reminder to herself as much as to him. Even as she declared them enemies, she ran her fingers into his thick hair and brushed a kiss on his mouth. She should step away, stop him now, but she wanted him with all her being. From the moment he touched her to slip his arm around her, it didn't matter that he was a Reed. It didn't matter that she was angry with him. Her decision to avoid kissing him had vanished like smoke in the wind.

What was important was that she was in his arms and he was showering her with light kisses, and in a minute, they would really kiss, another one of his heart-shattering kisses that she wondered if she would ever get over. At this moment that's all she wanted, more than anything else.

"We've always been enemies, but there's one place where we're in sync, compatible, consumed with mutual desire and intent. Right here. In each other's arms," he whispered, showering kisses on her face and throat. "You want me. I know you do. I can feel it, Claire." As he talked and kissed her lightly, he caught the red T-shirt in his hands and pulled it off to toss it away.

"Oh, Jake," she whispered, and he covered her mouth, stopping her protest that was only a whisper. Her arm was tight around his waist, and her other hand was tangled in his hair.

She moaned softly, longing raging for all of him. Common sense was a dim whisper, warning her that she was going to regret every minute of kissing and caressing him and letting him kiss and fondle her. She knew she should stop him now before she was hopelessly lost and in love with him and needing his hands and mouth and body as part of her life.

"Jake, I'm not going to do this."

"You want to kiss as much as I do," he whispered,

still showering kisses over her breasts as he unfastened her bra and tossed it away. He straightened to cup her breasts in his large, warm hands, and he was incredibly gentle, stroking her nipples so lightly with his thumbs, slow, light circles around the pink tips, stirring sizzles that she felt to her very core while he gazed at her with obvious desire.

"You're gorgeous, Claire. Absolutely beautiful, so perfect and soft," he said in a gravelly voice, his words just a whisper, but she heard him.

"You can't imagine what you do to me. I want you in my arms, in my bed," he said, still caressing her breasts while he leaned down to trail kisses down her throat.

Her heart pounded. Desire swamped her, heating her until she felt as if she stood in a blaze of fire. His hands, his mouth, his words, his kisses—all of them were seduction.

She longed to touch him, to kiss him, to have his hands and mouth on her. She wished he would keep kissing her and never stop.

She closed her eyes for an instant, ignoring the warnings that were clamoring in her thoughts, just yielding to his loving, letting her hands roam over his hard body. Only for a moment, she promised herself, and then she would stop him. She had to if she was going to survive. He would break her heart into a million pieces if she fell in love with him. If she let him make love to her, she knew she would be *in love* with him.

He was too sexy, had too much finesse. She would be swept away, lose her heart to him, a big, handsome, sexy cowboy neighbor, a man who understood her life, who respected her, a man who dazzled her, a man she might fall in love with forever. And that would be pain, heartbreak and hurt that could last a lifetime.

They were enemies, she reminded herself as she clung to his strong body and kissed him, surrendering herself to the most erotic kiss she had ever experienced. And ever would.

His mouth on hers swept her away, dazzled her, set her ablaze with longing for so much more. She didn't know how long they stood there in each other's arms, kissing and caressing each other, tension and need building.

"Jake," she whispered, catching his wrists in her hands and stepping back. "I have to stop. I'll be so in love with you, I will never get over it," she cried. "We not only have no future—your family will be furious."

He was looking at her as if he could devour her, and that made her heart pound more. His desire was obvious and intense. She wanted to step back into his embrace, kiss and caress him and forget every sensible warning.

She fought the urge to toss aside caution and put

her arms around him. Jake was fabulous, sexy, kind, intelligent, and his were the best kisses ever. But he was too appealing, a risk to her heart.

She thought about the hurt she would feel if she let herself fall in love with him. She wouldn't be able to walk away without leaving her heart behind. She had never been kissed the way Jake had kissed her. Fantastic, bone-melting, seductive kisses that just made her want more and more.

"Claire, let me do the worrying about my family," he whispered. "I know what I'm doing and what I want. You've been independent long enough to know what you want. And you're making what you want damn evident."

His words were seductive, too. They inflamed her, challenged her, and she felt caught and held by her own desires.

Desires that she knew could be her undoing.

It was the hardest thing she'd ever had to do, but she pulled back from his arms, immediately mourning the lack of his touch, and shook her head. "I can't do this."

He lowered his arms, and his eyes speared hers. The desire she saw in his expression made her feel that she was the most important woman on earth to him. He looked as if he wanted her with all his being and as if he was in love, but she knew better than that. He wasn't in love with her and never would be. She turned quickly, grabbing up her clothes. "This is what has to be," she said, holding her clothes against her. "You have to go, Jake."

He stood there without moving for seconds, his gaze piercing hers, and then, without saying one word, he turned and left her suite.

The urge to call him back was a powerful force, and she mustered all her self-control to fight it.

As she closed the door behind him, she leaned against the cool wood, but she wasn't aware of it. Drifting through memories of Jake, all she remembered were his hands, his mouth, his body, their kisses. Fantastic, sexiest-ever kisses that she would never forget. And her body felt as if it were on fire.

Her emotions held her captive as her thoughts battled each other. Did she really want him to stop? Or should she make love with Jake? He was the sexiest man she had ever known.

He had become incredibly desirable. She wanted him to make love to her. She wanted to make love to him, to discover his fascinating male body, to have his hands and mouth all over her.

She groaned and held her hands over her face. "No, no, no," she said aloud. She knew she shouldn't give in to those desires. Jake partied a lot on weekends. He had women in his life always, and he had never been serious about any of them.

He would not fall in love with her. Claire knew that absolutely. She thought their attraction was a fluke because she was staying with him and they had been caught up in the emotional struggle of the fires. And she thought he had been feeling sorry for her because of her loss and paid more attention to her than he ever would have otherwise.

Men like Jake did not fall in love with women like her. She was solitary, plain, led a life that a lot of men didn't like, although having her own ranch wouldn't bother Jake. But she wasn't his type of woman at all. Claire had seen him out enough in her life to know he liked gorgeous, outgoing women who were fun and sexy and would guarantee him a good time.

Jake was not a marrying man, so at some point, she risked a very broken heart.

Even if they were compatible, could she have a happy relationship with Jake with the family feud hanging over them and influencing everything they did?

Common sense said no, she could not have a good relationship with Jake. Not now, not later, not ever. Definitely, he was not the man for her. She should not get involved with him.

But did she really want to toss aside the chance of making love with him, of having the sexiest night— or nights—of her life with him? Would she look back with big regrets? If only she knew she could make love and then say goodbye to him, not get hurt, just move on, but she suspected if she yielded her body, her heart would be part of the deal.

"I may already be falling for you," she whispered,

her eyes still closed while she thought about him. "You're going to break my heart if I don't stop you."

She opened her eyes and mentally told herself she had to stop talking out loud to herself about him, because he had already overheard her once and she didn't want him to overhear her again.

She would probably already have lost her heart to him except for that streak of Reed in him where he could turn right around and annoy her. Like he had over that metal box.

"Dang, Jake," she whispered. She needed to get her mind on business, take care of the calls she had to make about her destroyed house and forget about him.

And she needed to find another place to stay and get out of his house before she surrendered to his seduction.

She got ready to go into town and left to find him.

When she stepped out onto the porch, she heard sounds of metal scraping metal, so she walked down the steps into the yard. Jake was hosing off the big metal box that he had said had belonged to his family. She felt annoyed that he was back on that again. At the same time, her heart beat faster as she looked at his broad-brimmed cowboy hat pushed back on his head, his locks of black hair falling in a tangle on his wide forehead. His jeans were tight on his long legs, his flat stomach and his narrow waist. He had shed his jacket, rolled up his blue denim sleeves and unbuttoned the first three buttons of his shirt.

She saw the tangle of black chest curls, his broad shoulders that made the sleeves of his shirt pull tightly when he leaned over the metal container and tried to clean it off. It was a dull silver, covered with dents and scratches, far cleaner now than an hour before.

She walked close, and he glanced at her and then went back to his task of cleaning the box. She looked down at it and saw the scratches and letters where he had cleaned the dirt and ash.

A few letters stood out clearly: a large straight line with a half circle that looked like the top of a capital *R*. She couldn't read the next letter because there were scratches, maybe an *X*. Then what looked like the lower part of an *E*, and she drew a deep breath. "I don't remember seeing these letters carved in this box before."

"Well, I damn sure haven't been out here carving my initials into the tin," he retorted. "But I sanded down some of the scratches that sort of hid what we have here. I drove back to my ranch house this morning. I needed to look things over anyway, but while I was there, I found my key to this box. I've been waiting to let you open it with my key."

"You haven't tried to open it?" she asked, more aware of the sunshine on his wide-brimmed tan hat that shaded his face, his muscled arms straining the fabric of his shirt and reminding her how it felt to be held in them. Also, she thought about Jake's kisses and for a few seconds forgot the metal box. She was annoyed, but at the same time her pulse raced, and she couldn't stop looking at his strong body, his very kissable mouth.

She wanted his arms around her. She wanted his kisses even while she was angry with him for still insisting her brothers had stolen the box from his family. She could try the key and put an end to his argument.

What if he was right? What if it was a box that had belonged to his family? She glanced again at the *R* that she could clearly read now.

She didn't want to worry needlessly until she knew it without question. She walked closer to him, holding out her hand while she looked into his thickly lashed dark eyes and thought he had bedroom eyes, dark eyes made for seduction. "I had a key at my house for this box, but that key is probably buried by ashes now."

"When we had this, there were three antique weapons we kept in it," he told her. "A Winchester rifle and two antique Colt revolvers."

Her eyes widened slightly, and she was startled, because those guns should still be in the box. That's what had been in there all the years her dad had had the box. He always said his dad had given it to him and his dad had owned it for years. She figured it had been her grandfather's until he gave it to her dad.

But how would Jake know the weapons that had been in their box? Could he be telling the truth? Would her brothers and her dad stoop to stealing something from Jake and then lie about it?

For the first time, she realized they might have done exactly that.

She looked up and met Jake's dark gaze, unfathomable eyes that hid his feelings.

"You know those guns are or were in that box," he said, and she could hear a tight note of anger in his voice. "Also, along with the old weapons was a Glock that belonged to me. I have my initials scratched on it."

Shocked, she realized he had been telling the truth. She raised her chin and nodded. "I still find it very difficult to believe that my family stole this box from your family. They didn't do things like that."

He gave her a look. "Are you going to open it? You have my key."

He was angry and she had been, too, but her anger had fizzled when he listed those old weapons. Had her brothers stooped to stealing this box? All those weapons except the Glock had been in the box. One of her brothers or her dad could have taken that gun.

There was only one way she was going to find out now. She took a deep breath and stepped closer to put the key in the lock and turn it. She was aware of Jake standing so close beside her. She was even more aware of the anger in his dark eyes.

Anger that might be justified.

Eight

The box was stirring up memories of Claire's ornery brothers and the things they had done. Jake couldn't keep from experiencing a low-burning anger. She had been so absolutely certain her brothers and her dad wouldn't stoop to taking that box from his family, but that's just what they had done.

As she knelt to unlock the box, he watched her jeans pull tautly over her trim butt. Her long legs were folded under her and that thick red braid hung to her waist, once again making him wonder what she would look like if all that red hair was combed out.

Even in his anger, desire still burned hot and strong. He didn't want to feel desire. This morning, dealing with that box, he didn't want to be tied in knots wanting her, but he was. She had always been his enemy, her clan the cause of the feud. She was stubborn and with an annoying family of a rotten dad and two rotten brothers. The younger brother, Laird, wasn't that bad. Even so, Claire still could melt Jake with a look or set him on fire with a touch.

He wanted her in his arms right now. He wanted to peel her out of those tight jeans that covered what might be the sexiest legs in Texas. Then he wanted to caress and shower kisses on them. He wanted them wrapped around him while he made love with her.

"Well, here goes," she said, giving him one more fleeting glance.

He was so lost in thoughts of making love with her while she had her long, long legs wrapped around him that he had almost forgotten the metal box.

And then she opened the lid and let it fall back away from her with a clang while they looked at a box filled with papers. To his disappointment, he didn't see any weapons of any sort. He didn't see any money. Just a mess of papers. He stepped closer and leaned down to look at old bank statements, old tax returns, faded letters and lists of horses that had been bought and sold.

"Well, there," she said, turning to look at him as she stood and placed her hands on her hips.

Annoyed, he took a step forward, reached down and scooped up an armload of papers. Beneath all the mess of papers, in the area he had uncovered, was a long Winchester rifle.

Claire stared down at the weapon. "Oh my word," she exclaimed, her cheeks flushing suddenly. "Jake, I apologize. This must have belonged to your dad, and my brothers…they took it. My dad had to have known where they got it."

It didn't make sense. He should be angry, but he didn't care about the box now or the old weapons. He had proved his point. Now he just wanted his arms around her, to pull her close and kiss her endlessly.

He took out some more papers and revealed the two Colt revolvers. "Well, you can have this metal box, but I want the old guns. The Glock is gone— probably one of your brothers has it. I don't care about the box, either. You keep it to store your papers. I just wanted you to know that it was my dad's."

"Well, you've got your antique weapons and I've got my old records. Actually, you can have the box. I'll buy a new one."

"You keep it. I'll take the weapons because they're collector's items," he said.

She looked down as she bit her lip. "Jake, I really am sorry for what my brothers did. It wasn't right to take these guns. I had no idea."

He draped his arm casually across her shoulders. "I believe you. And I don't want what our families did to keep following us."

She took a deep breath. "Yes, but we're still living with that feud. It'll never go away."

"We can do a whole lot to make it go away," he said softly, tightening his arm around her shoulders slightly to turn her toward him as he placed his other hand on her hip. His big smile was gone as he gazed at her with a solemn expression. Desire filled his dark eyes and made her pulse race faster. "It doesn't exist between us," he said in a husky voice. "We've already kissed it away." His hand on her shoulder moved to caress her nape, light strokes that made her want to kiss again.

She was highly aware of him touching her, of how close he stood and of how intently he looked at her. She wanted his kiss, longed for his arms around her. She forgot about the world, her resolutions to be more cautious about him. The old feud? She didn't think he was correct in saying they had gotten rid of it because of a few kisses. It could come storming back with more fury than ever if their relatives discovered them together, but right now, momentarily, where Jake was concerned, that feud didn't exist. She wanted to be held in his arms to kiss and be kissed.

When he leaned closer, her heart beat faster. "You can't imagine how much I want to kiss you right now," he whispered, brushing her lips with his, making her long for more of him. She wrapped her arms around him as his arm slipped around her waist and he held her against him. His other hand tangled in her hair while his mouth covered hers. Leaning over her to hold her tightly, he kissed her, his tongue going deep, slipping over hers, sending waves of desire through her that made her yearn for more of him, for his hands and mouth all over her.

She had never known a man as sexy as Jake. Warnings and caution disappeared, overruled by desire. She clung to him, kissing him in return while he held her in his tight embrace.

She ran her other hand over him, tossing back his hat to run her hand through his thick hair, down across his arm, down his back. She felt his fingers moving over her, and then he leaned away, and she opened her eyes to look up at him as he pulled her red T-shirt off to toss it away.

"Jake, we're outside. There isn't any privacy."

"There isn't anyone for the next five miles in any direction, but it won't matter," he said, picking her up easily and turning, taking the steps two at a time to the porch and then carrying her inside as he kissed her.

When his mouth covered hers, she closed her eyes and returned his kiss, forgetting her surroundings, lost in his kiss that made her long for more from head to toe. Giddy with his kiss and being carried in his arms, she held him tightly.

His kisses fanned desire until she wanted him desperately, immediately. As he stood her on her feet, she glanced around. They were in his big bedroom, standing near his bed. It gave her pause, and for a moment she felt that warning of caution set in. Did she want to stop him now before they went far beyond kisses?

She placed her hands on his face, looking up and gazing into his dark brown eyes that blazed with such intense desire that she lost some of her hesitation.

"Jake, I—" But she didn't get a chance to finish what she was about to say. Her words were stifled by his kiss. As he ravaged her mouth, he unfastened her bra and pushed it away. His big, callused hands cupped her breasts, and his thumbs lightly drew slow circles on her nipples until his lips trailed down and took over. His mouth captured one nipple, his tongue laving it to a hard pebble.

Sensations rippled through her, building her hungry need for his loving.

She knew if she intended to stop him, now was the moment. Did she want to take the risks to her heart that she knew Jake would cause?

She tunneled her hands through his hair. "Jake—" she whispered.

He looked up into her eyes and then leaned down, coming closer to put his mouth against her ear. "You want this," he whispered, his breath light, tickling her ear. "You want me inside you, hard and fast. I want to make love to you, and you want me to." As he talked, he shed his clothes, kicking off his boots and socks, peeling out of his jeans and briefs. He'd already shed his shirt.

When he stood before her, naked, she placed her hand against his chest. "Jake, I do want this. I want you. All of you." She reached down and captured his erection.

Wrapping his arms around her waist, he smiled at her. "Good, because you already feel how much I want you."

"I think you're the sexiest man alive. I shouldn't admit that to you because it can just go to your head…or other parts that might have a bigger reaction," she said as a smile flickered across her face.

"Come here, beautiful. I want to kiss you until we're both eager to move to the next stage." He reached out again to catch her wrist and draw her flush against him.

"I thought you'd never ask," she said as she went eagerly.

He kissed her neck lightly, arousing her more, driving her mad with need.

"You want my hands on you, don't you?" he asked her softly, his breath falling lightly on her ear. As he whispered, he cupped her breasts in his warm hands and ran his thumbs slowly over her nipples again, making her moan. She thrust her hips against him, wanting more, wanting him totally and completely. He met her need and made quick work of taking off her pants. His tender caresses made her tremble and shake as her need escalated.

"You didn't answer me. Do you want my hands on you? Touching you here?" he asked, caressing her breast. Bliss enveloped her while she clung to his hips and her gaze ran over his broad shoulders and chiseled chest. She wanted his hands on her, and he knew it.

"Yes, yes," she whispered, shoving aside the thought that she might have huge regrets later. "Right now, I want you all over me." She ran her fingers over his engorged manhood, stroking him, hearing his breath catch.

His body was male perfection, his manhood thick and ready. He rubbed slowly against her, just slightly, a sensual brush of their bare bodies. If he did that to make her more aware of both of them naked and holding each other, he succeeded. That contact was sexy, a body and legs caress that made her intensely aware of their nude bodies.

"Ahh, my darlin'," he whispered. "You have no idea what you do to me," he added as he kissed her throat. "You're beautiful, darlin'. Absolutely breathtaking," he whispered, his breath tickling her ear again. His words thrilled her while his caresses fanned desire into a fiery need for all of him, his tongue, his magic hands, his thick manhood that she could feel pressed against her now.

Still caressing her, he stepped back to take a long,

slow look at her. His gaze on her was incredibly
erotic, even more so than his touch. He was the lover
she thought he would be—deliberate, taking his time
to arouse her slowly, looking at her as if she were the
most gorgeous woman on earth.

He stepped close again, trailing kisses on her
breasts while he slipped his hands lightly down to
unfasten her jeans and push them off. When her jeans
fell around her ankles, she stepped out of them. She
wore her lacy pink panties. Watching her, he hooked
his fingers in her panties and slipped them down
slowly and then let them drift to her feet. As she
looked into his eyes, she stepped out of them while
he placed his hands on her hips.

"You're fabulous," he whispered. He wrapped his
arms around her and kissed her, one of his sizzling
kisses that made her shake.

He picked her up to place her on his bed and then
he knelt on the bed beside her, starting at her ankles,
running his fingers so lightly over her legs, drifting
up to her inner thighs while he trailed kisses where
his fingers had been.

He knelt between her legs and leaned down, running his hands lightly on her legs, his tongue trailing along her inner thigh. His tongue swept slowly
along her other thigh while his fingers rubbed between her legs. She arched to meet him as he stroked
her, erotic strokes that built her need. And then his

warm breath spilled over her as he ran his tongue over her intimately.

"Jake, I want you inside me," she gasped.

"Just wait," he whispered, sliding his fingers between her legs to stroke and rub her more, building tension.

"Jake, make love to me," she whispered, moving her hips as he continued to arouse her. "I need you."

"Oh, Claire, we're just getting started," he whispered, his breath hot on the place that yearned for him.

"Ahh, I want you," she cried, clinging to his strong arms, lost in sensations that increased her desire.

"You like that, don't you?" he whispered. "You want my tongue where my fingers have been, don't you?" She didn't answer him; she couldn't form the words. She could only feel her body come alive as he gave her what she wanted.

As his tongue continued to fondle her, building pressure and making her want him more by the minute, she gripped the sheets. Desire and need enveloped her. She gasped with pleasure, closing her eyes, moving her hips. As his hands and mouth played over her, she throbbed with the need to have him inside her right now.

She ran her fingers through his black curls, holding him against her, a sizzling tension building in her. When she thought she couldn't withstand the onslaught any longer, he pulled back from her, and her breath stalled. She watched him step off the bed to get a packet out of his jeans pocket and place it on the table beside the bed. He paused, and his gaze went slowly over her from head to toe as he got back on the bed and knelt between her legs.

She ran her fingers down his thighs as her gaze drifted over him. He was perfection. Broad shoulders, strong arms, chiseled abs, slim hips and a powerful erection. She wanted him with all her being. He had built the need inside her, and now she ached for him.

She sat up and caressed him, showering light kisses over his body just as he had kissed and teased her. Her hands ran over his fascinating strong body while his drifted so lightly over her. Then she lay back down and held out her arms to him.

"Come love me," she whispered.

As his arms wrapped around her, her heart beat faster. He leaned down, cupping one breast and stroking her nipple with his tongue. His wet tongue moved slowly, drawing circles, exciting her.

"Jake," she whispered, tingling, closing her eyes and shutting out everything except his hands on her and the feelings sweeping over her from his slow caresses that made her tremble with desire.

Suddenly, she wanted to hold him tightly and kiss him, one of those earth-shattering, unforgettable kisses that left her trembling and aching for more. Kisses to remember, if she wanted to, the rest of her life.

"Jake," she said again, this time holding his arms till he looked up at her and met her gaze. She slipped her arm around his neck to bring him down for a kiss. The second her tongue touched his, his arm tightened around her. He leaned over her, kissing her, his tongue stroking hers, his kiss passionate, building desire into a flaming need for both of them. Moaning softly, deep in her throat, she knew she had never been kissed like this. She wanted all of him for hours, his hands and mouth all over her. And at the same time, she thought she'd die if she didn't have him right then.

For a fleeting moment she had a strong feeling that this man would break her heart, but she also didn't want to stop kissing him. Jake's kisses and his loving were worth a risk to her heart.

As he kissed her and held her with his arm around her waist, his other hand slipped down her back to her bottom, lightly stroking her, caressing her and then leaning away to slide his hand down her belly and between her legs, his fingers toying with her, arousing her more.

She thrust her hips toward him to give him easier access, spreading her legs farther apart while they kissed, and his hand drifted so lightly over her. His intimate strokes built her need for all of him.

She had made her commitment and now savored

his kiss. He took her breath away with his handsome looks, and now his touch made her desperate for so much more of him.

"You're gorgeous. So incredibly sexy to me. I want you, darlin'. I want you with all my being," he said in a gruff whisper. "I want to know every beautiful inch of you," he said, his voice growing huskier as he sheathed himself.

Even though she didn't believe that she was that fascinating to him, his words thrilled her. "Jake, I want you, too," she said, her gaze raking over his powerful body, his stiff erection. "I want you inside me now."

She reached up to lock her hands behind his neck and pull him down for a kiss. He moved over her and lowered himself carefully, a weight she welcomed while she ran her hands over his back, down across his trim, firm butt.

His body was muscular, powerful and so totally masculine that she became oblivious to everything except his kisses, their tongues touching. Desire built, filling her, making her want him with a desperation she hadn't known before. He must have sensed how close she was, because he moved between her thighs and slid his broad hands beneath her to raise her hips to give him more access.

"Jake."

As she clung to him, she arched her back, raising

up to meet him as he entered her. Finally. She nearly cried out with pleasure and need.

His strokes were slow, light, meant to build tension, not offer release. As he moved over her, his gaze raked her.

"You don't know what you do to me," he said, his voice a hoarse whisper.

Her heart pounded with excitement, with a blinding need to achieve climax. His manhood was thick, filling her, and she spread her legs wider.

"Claire," he whispered. "I want to make it last."

She moaned as he thrust inside her again, slow and deep. She didn't know how much longer she could take what his body was doing to hers.

"Put your legs around me," he whispered in her ear, and she did, running her hand over his smooth back as he withdrew slowly and entered her again.

"Jake," she cried, arching her hips, holding him tightly, wanting him deep inside, moving with her.

He took his time now, withdrawing, then filling her until she was arching against him, crying out for him. Then he finally began to pump faster, and she moved with him. They rocked together, hard and fast, while he tried to keep control, to pleasure her as long as he could.

She thrust beneath him, matching his rhythm, clinging to him and arching against him as desire overwhelmed her.

"Jake!" she cried, holding him tightly as he gave

one final thrust that carried her to a peak and gave her sweet release.

Clutching him, moving her hips against him, she cried out in ecstasy while he pumped wildly, reaching his climax.

They both sank onto the bed. He held her tightly in his embrace while they gasped for breath. He turned his head to shower light kisses on her face.

"That," he whispered, "was the best. The absolute best."

She barely heard his words as she held him and tried to catch her breath. He had been everything she thought he would be. Her orgasm had been longer, hotter, better than ever before. But Jake had surprised her. As they lay together, he stayed hard, and before her heartbeat could slow down, he started pumping again and she reached the second climax, crying out with passion. She collapsed in his arms, held tightly while they both gulped for breath. As they began breathing quietly, she turned her head to kiss his cheek lightly, his stubby whiskers tickling her lips.

"I can't move," she whispered.

"I think that's my line," he said. He turned to look at her, kissing her forehead, the corner of her mouth, her ear. "You're fantastic." He moved to pull out of her, but she stopped him.

"Ahh, Jake. Just hold me close. I can hear your heart beating. I want you to stay with me."

"I'm with you. Ah, darlin'. I can't move. My bones melted."

She smiled. "I hope so. I wanted it to be good for you, because it was fantastic for me. Now, just hold me close. I don't want to move."

"I don't want you to move. This is perfect," he said, sounding content. She felt cherished, important to him, held against his warm body that was damp with sweat.

No matter what lay ahead, she would never regret making love with him, because he was the best possible lover. And how much had she fallen in love with him because of that? She couldn't answer her own question.

She was held tightly in his arms, their heartbeats and breathing returning to normal while she still tingled all over. She had been right in every way in thinking about what it would be like to have Jake make love to her. He was the consummate lover, fabulous, carrying her out of this world. Each climax had been earth-shattering.

She'd had lovers before in her life—only two, because she had met few men that really tempted her. Jake's kisses had been the sexiest ever, melting her resistance, and her climax had been paradise. She couldn't answer her own question, but she suspected when she shared her body, she'd given him part of her heart. She might be a little bit in love with him, and she would just have to live with that and hope she could get over it, because she had no illusions about his feelings.

He held her close their breath mingled. He was warm, his body solid, so fascinating to her.

He rolled over to prop his head on his hand, looked down at her and smiled. He ran his index finger slowly along her jaw and up to her ear. "I want to keep you here in my bed the rest of the month."

"Well, you can't do that, but I can stay awhile. Later, I need to get back to getting my ranch back in order and everything rebuilt. Sometimes that overwhelms me——everything that needs to be rebuilt. Barns, corrals, fences, my house, other houses, an office. So much to build from just ashes. I really appreciate getting to stay here."

He smiled. "Believe me, you can't appreciate being here as much as I'm happy to have you here. You take your time. There's no rush for you to rebuild and get out."

"Thank you," she said, smiling at him.

"I want you with me. This is a fabulous time," he said, showering light kisses on her throat and then turning her to kiss her again, another deep kiss that stirred desire far sooner than she expected.

An hour later, they were still in bed, and she was in his arms, her naked body pressed against his as he held her close.

"Jake, I was going to town to get some clothes. Also, I need to call all sorts of people about my house and property and get work started on rebuilding. First, I have an appointment with my insurance agent."

"It'll all be there when you do call, and right now they're swamped anyway. Relax and let's enjoy the most fabulous lovemaking ever," he said, his voice growing husky as it did when he thought about making love. "I want you here in my arms, against my body for just a bit longer. What time we wasted. I should have had you as a guest long, long ago and gotten to know you."

She smiled. "After this we should be able to settle our differences out of court, huh?"

"Let's not talk about ranches and differences and problems today," he said while he ran his fingers over her bare shoulder and then down to her breast. "This is a special time." He leaned closer to kiss her lightly on her throat, trailing more kisses over her jaw. "You're beautiful. I can never get enough of looking at you naked."

She wondered if she was already in love with him. She couldn't think about it rationally when she was in his arms with his hands drifting over her.

He held her close now, still running his fingers over her.

"Claire, I want you to stay while you get your house rebuilt. You don't have a home on your ranch or any outbuildings, and you can't throw up a tent until that land is cleared of debris. Stay here with me. That will give us some time together, because when you go back, when we step back into our regular lives, you know our lives won't be the same as they are now."

She shook her head. "No, they won't be the same. And I don't think you've thought through your invitation to me," she said, smiling at him. "I can't get a new house thrown up in a few weeks. That project will take months."

"I know what I'm asking," he said solemnly, and her heart thumped. Stunned by the unexpected invitation to stay a long time with him, she gazed into his dark eyes while her heart beat faster at the thought of weeks in his arms, in his bed, making love often.

"I'll have to think about that one," she answered quietly. "If I stay a long time with you, it will become known in these parts. That could cause an uproar with all my relatives. It could cut me out of my family. I don't want that to happen. I'm trying to reconnect with them. I have to think about that. It's not going to go over well with your family, either. I know you have relatives in Texas, although not close to here, and you know that I do also."

"We run a risk, but I don't think my family will cut me out."

"I don't want to lose my family, but they probably saw my house burn on television. They might yield a little because of my losses. I can't guess. I'll have to think about the risk I take. Also, my brothers may try to catch you alone where they can beat you up for letting me stay here."

"Let me worry about that one. I'll be careful, and I'm not scared of your brothers."

"On the other hand, I need to be near my property to rebuild. I don't have another place to stay. This is perfect for me to work with the contractors on building a new house."

Her breath stilled as she thought of another reason to rethink staying at Jake's cabin.

"Then there's another risk if I stay. I want to say yes right now, while at the same time, common sense tells me if I stay with you and we keep making love, I'll never want to leave you. I'll fall so deeply in love with you, my heart will break when we part. I don't know. I have to give your offer thought before I answer."

"Think about it. I don't think you'll fall in love. You're incredibly independent, accustomed to running your own ranch. You'll just go back to your regular routine."

She suspected he was describing himself and his reactions to staying with someone he had had sex with and then said goodbye.

"I'm not sure you know what you're asking. It's none of my business, so if you don't want to answer, don't. My guess is that you've never invited someone to stay with you that long."

He shook his head. "No, I haven't, but it's different this time. You don't even have a house. You'll be gone a lot on your ranch, supervising and working and just here at night—the best time and when I'm home. You're damn independent or you wouldn't be living over there alone and running that ranch. I think we can work it out, and if we can't, we'll change the arrangements."

She smiled. "You promise to ask me to leave if you get tired of me?"

He gazed back solemnly. "I can't imagine asking you to leave for a long time. I'm not a marrying man, Claire, but I want you here with me. And for the record, I don't think you're a marrying woman, either."

She shook her head as she smiled. "Not to a Reed. You're safe there, Jake. I've told you my feelings on that, and I know you wouldn't ever want to marry a Blake. You lost a brother because of his marriage to a Blake. I lost a sister. So you're right. I won't want to marry you. But that doesn't mean I won't fall in love with you and end up with a broken heart."

"I think you're safe on that one after what you just told me. So you'll stay?" he asked, staring intently at her and sounding as if he really wanted her at his house on his ranch. She was shocked and stared at him while she thought about it.

"I don't have anywhere to go except Dallas, and I need to be out here right now to get things back into a routine. I'll stay here if you will promise—

absolutely be honest about it—that you will tell me to leave if you want me out of here."

"I promise," he said instantly, smiling at her and sounding happy, as if she had just given him a wonderful gift. She gazed at him and wondered about what she was getting into. If they fit together as well the rest of the time as they had the past twenty-four hours, she wouldn't want to leave. At the same time, she wouldn't ever want to marry him, because that would be a disaster.

Another thought hit her. Could Jake fall in love with her? Was he so certain his heart was safe, and he couldn't be hurt, or were they both going to end up heartbroken?

Nine

A few hours later, Claire faced Jake and knew she would never view him the same way she had before they made love too many times to count. Her feelings about him had made a monumental change. Could they stay on a friendly basis? How much would their lovemaking improve their neighborly relationship? How much did she care about him now?

She glanced over at the clock and gasped. "Jake, do you know that it's after three in the afternoon?" she said, turning to him as he rolled over to face her and prop his head on his hand. As he smiled at her, she brushed locks of black hair off his forehead.

"I don't really care what time it is. I don't want

to leave this bedroom yet. This has been fabulous," he said.

"It's time, Jake. We've been here all night and all morning, going into the afternoon. It's been fabulous, but it's time to go back into our real world, back to the problems, because I really want to go into town and get some clothes."

"I know you're right." He placed his hand on her arm lightly. "Before we go, I have a question—actually an invitation. We're having a celebration. It's a thank-you dinner Saturday night in Dallas for people who contributed to rebuilding the arena. My cousins and I made a generous donation, and I want you to go with me."

A cold chill suddenly ran down her spine as the world intruded on their idyll.

"We're naked in bed together—I don't think you thought that invitation through. I would love to go with you, but how can we go out in public in Dallas? We could easily run into Reeds or Blakes and all hell would break loose. Besides, it will stir things up for some locals to see a Reed out with a Blake, and you know it. We can ignore some things, but there's no reason to go asking for trouble and for you to take me to an event. I think that's looking for trouble. Worse, disaster."

He shook his head. "This dinner should be okay. They've had several of these thank-you get-togethers, where they report on the progress of the construction, and my cousins have never once come. It's a small group going to a private club, and we'll be in our own room. There's a chance to run into relatives, but it isn't likely. Like I said, I don't remember any Blakes or Reeds that will be at this shindig. We'll just go in my limo, be shut away in a private room and then get back into the limo to go to my apartment in Dallas. The chances are slim."

"And you're willing to take that risk?" she asked.

"I want to take you, so yes, I'm willing to take the risk. I don't think it's likely I'll see any relatives. Frankly, I don't see many of my relatives in Dallas. They're more in Amarillo and scattered in smaller towns, and they don't go to Dallas a lot. There's always that chance we'll see someone, but I think we can deal with it. I'm willing to take the risk and live the way I want to live. It should be a fun evening, and you seemed interested in the arena." As he talked, his fingers ran over her arm and the back of her hand. Then he moved his hand to caress the nape of her neck. Each light caress kept her thoughts on him more than thinking about going out with him and the problems that could mean.

"You know I want to go with you," she admitted honestly.

"Good. So, you'll do it. I'll try to see to it that you have a fun evening," he drawled, and she smiled, shaking her head.

"It didn't take you long to talk me into it. Before

we go to the party, though, I really should spend a day in Dallas. I need something to wear, I need my hair done—you know, girl stuff. I'm going to have to get a new pickup and a new car sometime, but I want to go to Dallas for that, too, and I can't go today."

"We can go to Dallas Thursday or Friday and stay in my apartment. I'll get my pilot to fly us to Dallas. You can get ready and do what you want to do during the day. Just leave the nights for me."

"Let's go on Thursday, and I can get some business done," she said, amazed to be planning her life and including him in it. "I'll make appointments, because I have to see about the insurance and a lot of things on clearing my land and rebuilding my ranch house and replacing my vehicles. We moved a lot of things before the fire, so it shouldn't be too much. We've got a routine for emergencies and it worked to save a lot of equipment. Trouble is, you can't move everything. I can get my pickup, and then you won't have to drive me around."

"Come here," he said in a husky voice, reaching out to lift her closer against him as he wrapped his arms around her. Held against his nude body, looking into his sexy, long-lashed dark eyes, she forgot about the weekend, the problems, the things she needed to do. She just wanted his kisses, his loving, their bodies joined. The more they kissed and made love, the more she wanted him. Would she fall in love with him?

If she did, he would break her heart, because she was certain Jake wasn't falling in love. He wanted hot sex, endless hours of loving, but she suspected part of him was locked away, not to be shared, and he wasn't ever going to be in love. And if the impossible happened and he fell in love with her, that would disrupt both their lives and tear them away from their families. She didn't want that, either. There was no good solution to a relationship with him. And she knew she better face that fact and keep a realistic outlook with realistic expectations. Getting involved with Jake Recd meant disaster whatever way she went.

No matter how fabulous and exciting sex was between them, how compatible they had become, at some point, they would have to say goodbye.

"I think it's time for me to dress—in my same old jeans and in one of your T-shirts. Then let's go into Persimmon and get me some other clothes."

"Whenever you're ready," Jake replied, though if he had his choice, he'd keep Claire naked and in bed for the rest of the day and into the night. "I will say, those jeans you've been wearing still look mighty good on you," he added with a wink.

"Thank you. But I'm ready for new ones. Now, what are we going to do about riding into town together—a Blake and a Reed in the same car? That will turn everyone upside down."

"I'll drop you off at my uncle Bernard's hardware store. The family avoids it unless they desperately need some hardware because he's such a grump."

"He is that, I'll agree, but I figured it was just with my family. That's kind of funny that he is with his own family. Well, he'll still see us and spread the word."

"He might, but it's unlikely. He doesn't pay attention until someone corners him and says they want to buy something."

She smiled and nodded. "Okay. We'll see what happens. I suppose you'll pick me up there, too."

"Might as well. I'll be parked and waiting if you can give me an approximate time."

"Sure. Give me an hour."

"That's not a lot of time."

"Persimmon isn't a big place, and they're limited on what they have. It won't take long because I'm not particular and I'm a fast shopper. Just in case, an hour and fifteen minutes."

"Sounds good to me. Like Scotty's Burgers? If you do, I'll have two when I come get you."

"That would be nice. Now I need to get dressed."

"Can I help?"

She smiled as she shook her head. "I think not. We might not get to town at all if you help."

"Might not, but I'll bet you'd have more fun."

"I can't argue that one," she said as she wiggled away.

He put his hands behind his head to watch her as

she got out of bed. She was nude, gorgeous, and he wanted her again. She yanked the top sheet off the bed, wrapped herself in it quickly and started out of the room as he reached for her, but she did a quick step and dodged his hand.

"Claire, come here," he coaxed in a husky voice.

She shook her head. "No, no. We're sticking to our plan. You promised to take me to Persimmon for clothes, and we're not putting that off any longer. We've already made love for hours. See you on the porch." She rushed out of his room and closed the door behind her.

Smiling, he got up to take a cold shower. He needed it. They had made love for hours, but he couldn't get enough of her, and the sight of her nude made him want her just as much as if they hadn't loved at all.

That was a new one for him. In fact, he thought, several things about her were different from his experiences with other women. Not being able to get enough of her was one. He wanted her even more now than he had before their first kiss. And, he didn't want her to go home—in this case, she didn't have her ranch home to go back to, so he might get that wish. Claire wasn't like any other woman he had ever known—independent, a rancher and a damn good one. On top of that, she just might be the sexiest woman he had ever known—that was the real shocker.

Just thinking about her made him want to go find her and peel her out of her clothes and make love again before they left for town. He knew she wouldn't go for it, but that's what he would like to do, and he was shocked by his own feelings. How much was she going to tie him up in knots and change his life?

After an hour in Persimmon, Claire went back to where they agreed to meet. She had new jeans, new socks and sneakers, new underwear and T-shirts in bags and boxes. She saw Jake sitting in the driver's seat of his pickup, his feet on the dash, his head back on the seat.

She put her head in the open window and leaned close to his ear. "Hey, Sleeping Beauty, I'm back," she whispered.

As his eyes opened, his arm slipped around her shoulders. He pulled her closer.

"Jake—" she started to protest. He drew her head down, covered her mouth with his and ended whatever she had been about to say.

His tongue stroked hers, and she forgot everything else, forgetting where she was, what she had been doing, everything except Jake, his mouth on hers in a kiss that made her want to keep on kissing. Finally, she wiggled away slightly, but he kept his arm around her.

"Jake, wait—we're on Main Street. Do you want

all our relatives to know we have a truce? And they will hear about it."

"I think you started this," he said in a lazy drawl. "Get in this pickup with me and I'll finish it," he added, making her want him more than ever, even though she laughed.

"I should have known better than to walk up and whisper in your ear like that," she told him. He opened his arms, and she slipped away, walking around to get into the passenger side.

"My brothers will hear about us," she said as she buckled her seat belt, "so watch your back."

"I promise you—I'm not scared of your brothers. I'll take one of my cowboys as a bodyguard," he smiled.

"I'm serious! Please be careful. I'm sure someone saw us."

"You didn't buy anything?" he asked, sitting up.

She motioned to the back seat, and he glanced over his shoulder. "Ahh, that should do it for a couple of days." His gaze went over her. "Nice duds. You look great."

She laughed. "Thank you, but I'm wearing the same clothes I wore when we came to town. Those new ones get washed first. Anyway, for now, I'm finished shopping."

"You were speedy. I brought the burgers about ten minutes before you arrived. Do you want to go to the park and eat them or just sit here in the car?"

"The park. Unless there are lots of people there. Let's go see. It's a pretty day, and we can sit under a tree and I can enjoy my burger."

"I can think of some more fun things to do, but for that I suspect you would want more privacy than the park would provide."

"Yes, I think so," she said, smiling at him.

"And then back to my ranch," he said, starting his pickup.

"Yes, you'll still have a houseguest." Even as she said the words, she couldn't help thinking that she should just go to Dallas, get out of his ranch house, away from him. But once again, she thought how much easier it would be if she stayed at his place to meet people when they came out to keep all the appointments she had set up for the construction of her new ranch house and buildings. She already had four appointments.

"It's easier for you to get things done on your ranch if you're staying on mine, right there next to yours instead of driving out from Dallas every time," he said as if he knew what she was thinking.

"Oh yes. It's a lot more convenient," she answered. But she couldn't deny the truth she felt deep inside. There was another reason she wanted to stay with him: she wanted to be with Jake, in his arms again. Because she knew that's what would happen when they got back home.

* * *

On Thursday they flew to Dallas and Jake took Claire to her house, a large two-story in an old part of town. The area was full of multimillion-dollar mansions that had increased in value through the years and still boasted choice properties with large tree-shaded lawns, carefully tended flowerbeds and quiet streets. "Want to come inside and see my home?" she asked when the limo he'd hired pulled into her drive.

"I will when I pick you up. I know you have appointments. I'll be back Saturday night to get you for dinner at six. Sunday we go back to the ranch."

"Thanks, Jake. It'll help get started on my house if I can stay at your place and be right there when the contractors have questions. Once they begin to get it framed in, I can go home."

"I'm in no hurry to get you out of my house," he said.

"Oh my," she said in a breathless voice. "That sounds as if you want me in your bed a long time."

"Do I ever," he said. He slipped his arm around her waist. "You're teasing. I'm not. I want you and I want you in my bed." He kissed away her reply, and when he released her, she was breathless, all her teasing remarks forgotten. She fanned herself.

"Wow, you're one sexy man," she whispered. "I need to go inside and climb into the freezer to cool down."

"Instead, get your shopping done so I can take you to dinner and then to bed."

True. He reminded her she still had to find a dress for the arena celebration. "That's a deal, my handsome friend."

She watched him walk to the waiting limo, get in and disappear down the street. With a sigh she closed the door. "I still think you'll break my heart, but for now I am thoroughly enjoying the sexiest kisses ever," she whispered. "And the best possible sex."

She tingled at the thought of getting dressed up and going out for a night with him, something where they weren't in jeans, she wasn't in his giant T-shirts and wearing singed boots. Instead, she'd look more like the women he usually took out.

"Just wait, Jake. I'm about to give you a night to remember."

Saturday evening Jake stood at Claire's door after ringing the bell and waiting. He wore a charcoal suit, a red tie, gold links in his French cuffs and his best black boots.

When the door opened, he turned. "Are you—" He stopped as he stared in surprise. If he had been in public, somewhere besides her front door, and simply run into her, he wouldn't have known her.

He could only stare, and for a rare moment in his life he was speechless. He didn't even realize he wasn't speaking and hadn't greeted her. She was stunning, and he couldn't get his breath. Her red hair, parted in the center, framed her face as it fell over her shoulders. He thought about the long, thick braid she'd always had. Now her hair was only shoulder length, a beautiful dark red with streaks of blond highlights near her face.

Her sleeveless dress was a red silk that had a high, round collar, a belted midsection that showed her tiny waist and a straight skirt that went to midcalf that showed off every curve. She wore red platform sandals with high, thick heels, and he could only stare because his normally plainly dressed rancher neighbor took his breath away. She was so gorgeous. The red dress had a seam in front from chin to the hem. It wasn't very noticeable, but he saw it and realized it might be a zipper. He promised himself that before the night was over, he would know if it was a zipper. That thought made him wonder what she wore under the red dress.

"You look fantastic," he said.

"Thank you. You clean up rather well yourself," she said, smiling at him. "What a handsome devil you are, dear neighbor. My, oh my."

"That's what I say. Damn, you're gorgeous. I think I'd rather cancel the evening and take you to bed. Too bad I can't cancel. But I can't stop staring at you, either. You're stunning."

As she turned to get her purse, she glanced over her shoulder and smiled. "Thank you. That's nice to hear. And you look good enough to kiss, except we won't now because I don't want to get the least bit messed. I have spent the entire day working for this look, and I want a few minutes to enjoy it intact."

"Yes, ma'am," he said politely with laughter in his eyes. "I'm curious, though. Your hair isn't the same length. Did you get a haircut? Or were you wearing a fake long braid?" he teased.

"I got a haircut. I didn't need that much hair, but it was definitely mine."

"I can't stop looking at you."

She smiled at him. "I hope not. That's one goal I hoped to achieve. I wanted to get your attention," she said and meant it. She wanted him to see her in a dress, some way other than as he usually did on the ranch, and especially this last week after all they'd gone through. She wanted this night out, and she had already gotten a reaction from him that made the effort worthwhile. She felt the same way looking at him. He looked so incredibly handsome. He took her breath away. She looked forward to the night out with him, and it was a good cause. Even though her family was angry with his family that they had bought the property first, she loved that old arena and was glad they had rebuilt.

"You've got my attention, all right. You've got my brain's attention and you've got another area's attention, too. If we have an earthquake or typhoon, get me moving, because I won't notice it for looking at you."

"No typhoons, no earthquakes in the forecast, but I'll let you know if one happens."

"Let's go. As soon as I feel we can politely leave tonight, we will. I want to take you home with me."

"You don't have to do that here in Dallas. My Dallas home hasn't burned."

"I want you with me all night, in my arms, in my bed, where I can kiss every gorgeous inch of you. Okay?"

"More than okay," she replied in a sultry voice, wanting to be with him, in his arms, in his bed. "I can't wait to be with you later," she said softly, her voice getting that breathy quality that she couldn't avoid.

"To be truthful, I want you to show me what's under that gorgeous red dress."

"I'll do my best to oblige," she said, smiling at him.

"Maybe we should skip this party," he said, studying her and sounding as if he meant it.

"No, we won't. Stop trying. And we're not leaving early. Not after what I paid for this dress, these shoes and my hair. Not to mention my new undergarments that you get to remove later."

"Dang. That isn't the way to ensure you'll get to stay there long. That just makes me want to carry you off to bed now."

"I just wanted you to know that I'm looking forward to later, but I want to go to the party now. Besides showing off my new clothes, this is for a really good cause. And I will have an evening with the most handsome man in Texas, and that is saying a lot."

He smiled. "Thank you, my darling. Okay, let's hit the road."

Smiling, she picked up her envelope purse that matched her dress, closed the door and put the key into her purse.

"You'll come home with me tonight, won't you?" he asked.

"If you want, or you can come back here with me."

"Come home with me. I'll get you home when you're ready." He couldn't wait for the evening to be over. He'd seen women he'd taken out who had new dresses, new hairstyles, gorgeous women who looked like they'd stepped off the pages of a glossy fashion magazine, but Claire had undergone the biggest change and the most beautiful one.

He can't believe he didn't realize how beautiful she was before. She was a good-looking woman, and now she was drop-dead gorgeous, and he was stunned how good she looked. He knew she worked on her ranch. Her clothes were practical for that. Her long braid had been practical for being out in the dust and the wind with horses or cattle. But this transformation was astonishing. And he knew what a gorgeous body was under that red silk dress.

He realized she was staring at him. "I'm sorry. Did you say something to me?"

She laughed. "A penny for your thoughts. That isn't what I said, but I'm wondering what carried you away."

"You did. I can't get over how you look. I know you usually are dressed the best way to work on your ranch, but there is a vast difference between how you look on the ranch and how you look tonight."

She smiled. "I must be scary on the ranch."

"You're not a damn bit scary. You look good on the ranch. Haven't I conveyed that I thought you looked great?"

"As a matter of fact, yes, you have. I'm glad you think so tonight, too. I would hate to have gotten my hair cut and you not notice."

"Oh, lady. Every guy in the place is going to notice. I may hang on to you, so they know you're with me and don't come over to flirt with you."

She laughed. "That's not going to happen."

"I would win placing a bet on that one. Let's go so we can get through the evening and go home," he said, taking her arm lightly, looking intently at her and turning to walk to the limo with her.

The ride was quick, and before he knew it the driver held the limo door for them and Jake took her arm as they walked into the tall building, where the club was on the twentieth floor. As they entered the room, a man played the piano softly in a far corner.

Tables were set, but no one was seated yet. A cocktail party was going on, and people were on the balcony as well as inside.

They moved around the room to greet guests, and Jake saw that, like the last dinner, the room was filled with guys he'd ridden with and competed against in rodeos, which didn't surprise him, because they were the ones who were the most interested in the new arena. He also noticed the attention Claire was getting from every male in the room.

"My friend Stefanie Grant just arrived," Claire said, calling Jake's attention.

He looked around and saw the woman.

"I'll tell you, Stefanie does know how to make an entrance. She looks damn good, too, tonight."

"She told me who to call to get my hair done. It's the same group she goes to."

"Ahh. I'm glad you took her advice. Damn good advice. Stefanie always looks good. She could fall in the pigpen and look good."

Claire smiled. "I'll tell her you said that."

Jake grinned as he looked beyond her. "Her brother may be here someplace. There are a bunch of donors now, and this party is for all of us. My cousins—there were four of us who donated money. Since Cal died, there are just three of us involved actively now. Wade Sterling is one and he's supposed to be here tonight, although I don't see him now. One of the cousins lives in Colorado, and he hasn't been to any of these dinners till tonight. It's Luke Grayson. His wife and child were killed in a car wreck, and he hasn't been able to come."

"That's awful. I'm so sorry."

"Luke grew up here. He was a backyard neighbor of the Grants."

"I'm sorry to hear about his loss. Speaking of—here comes Stef. She called when she heard about the fire and wanted to know if I was all right. When she found out my home burned, she offered to let me stay in one of her empty houses in Dallas, which was nice of her. She owns Grant Realty, in case you didn't know."

"I know the Grants, and everybody knows Stefanie. Her brother, Noah, and I are friends."

He paused as a slender black-haired woman in a sleeveless black cocktail dress walked up and greeted them. She turned to Claire. "I'm so sorry about your ranch, your house and the other buildings."

"Thanks, Stefanie. The fire was dreadful."

"What about your ranch, Jake?" Stefanie asked, turning to him.

He shook his head. "I was enough to the east that the fire didn't get there. The wind drove it west and then north. If you ladies will excuse me, I see some friends I want to greet." As he walked away, Stefanie turned back to Claire.

"My, oh my, does he clean up good."

Claire gave Jake a lingering look. "I think I said the same thing to him. Yes, he does."

"So do you. Wow. You look absolutely gorgeous.'"

"You look gorgeous yourself. You always turn heads," Claire said. "Thank you so much for recommending the salon and who to book with. I'm really pleased with the outcome. So is Jake."

"I think they're great."

"I need to see you more often. I needed a lift after losing my home and all my things."

"Aww, Claire, I'm so sorry. I couldn't imagine," Stefanie said. Then she brightened. "You said you're staying at a neighbor's house. You didn't say which neighbor. But you didn't have to," Stefanie said, her eyes twinkling. "A Reed and a Blake? I hope those brothers of yours don't show."

"You couldn't drag them into any event honoring ranchers and cowmen and the like. No danger there, and Jake didn't seem to think we would run into his family, so here we are."

Stefanie smiled. "Jake's a nice guy."

"We're doing better than when we've gone to court to fight each other," Claire said, smiling at her friend. "I hope it lasts." Then she remembered what Jake had said. "Oh, by the way, Jake wanted me to pass on a compliment. He said you could fall into a pigpen and still look good."

Stefanie laughed. "Oh my. Tell him thank you for that lovely thought."

"Are you here with someone? May I ask who?"

"Sure, you can always ask. I came with Billy, and I think it will be the last time. I don't know why, but I just don't have the knack for finding the right guy. We argued all the way here…" She waved her hand. "But enough about that."

"I'm sorry, Stef."

"Not to worry, girlfriend. I'm not giving up hope." In an obvious attempt to deflect the conversation from her love life—or lack thereof—she said, "Well, like I said on the phone, I can always find a place for you to stay, Claire, with me or in a vacant house, so let me know if you need a place. Although if I were staying with Jake, I think I'd just settle in until the last inch of your ranch is fixed and ready."

Claire laughed. "I'll remember your advice. If the two of us fell wildly in love, though, there wouldn't be a future with that old feud. If it were like Regina, I wouldn't want that, either."

Stefanie frowned. "I think you're right. Like Romeo and Juliet."

Claire laughed. "That's a first. Later, I'll tell Jake that you called us Romeo and Juliet." She hoped their story wouldn't be as tragic, but she was sure Jake would find the humor in it. "By the way, how's your family?"

"Everyone's good. I'm an aunt again, and that's so much fun."

Claire smiled at a story her friend related, then

when they were about to part, she said, "I hope you have a good time tonight."

"I hope you have a good time, too. Jake seems nice. I hope your brothers know nothing about him."

"When they see me with him, I think they'll know better than to interfere. They may be rotten to some people, guys mostly, but they've never been rotten to me."

"Oh, here Billy comes, looking for me. I'll go so you don't have to talk to him and have him ask you why you're here with a Reed. He might not have noticed yet, but he's friends with some of the Reeds. Let's do lunch when you can," she said over her shoulder, and Claire nodded, watching Stefanie's black hair swing as she walked away.

"Claire?"

She turned to see one of the men involved with the arena and smiled at him. "Brink. This is a nice party, and I'm so glad a new arena will be built."

"I am, too. I almost didn't recognize you. You look great," he said. "Was that your house I saw on the news?"

"There were several houses on the news, but yes, the fire went across my ranch and my home is gone," she said, turning as another rancher joined them. She glanced across the room as she talked and saw Jake looking at her as he stood in a group of people, laughing at something someone said, but his eyes were on her, and she felt a tingle just from their exchanged glances. It was another twenty minutes of conversation before a hand touched her elbow and she looked up at Jake.

"Sorry to interrupt," he said, greeting the men standing around her. After he had shaken hands with each one, he looked down at Claire. "It's about time for this to start. If you gentlemen will excuse us, they're asking everyone to find their places."

He held her arm lightly as they moved away from the group. "I know where our places are. We're at the head table. I see Stefanie found you. So have half the guys in the room. You drew a crowd."

She smiled. "Friendly people. Ranchers. I'm a rancher."

"That isn't why you had eight guys standing around talking to you," he said, and she smiled.

"They've asked some of us to find our places because then everyone will," he told her. "So let's find our seats so we will get to eat dinner and get this shindig over with so I can take you home with me and see what's under your red dress."

"Sounds like a deal to me," she said, smiling at him and anxious for the time when she could return to his place and be alone with him.

As they reached the head table, two tall men and a woman were waiting. Jake greeted them and turned to her. "I want all of you to meet my ranch neighbor Claire Blake. Claire, these are my cousins, who have also helped with the building of the new arena in Fort Worth after the old one burned. This is Wade Sterling and his new wife, Ava Sterling."

Smiling, Claire greeted the Sterlings.

"I've heard a lot about you. I'm glad you two have a truce," Wade said.

"I'm glad, too," she said, smiling in return.

"And this is another cousin, Luke Grayson."

"I'm glad to meet you, Luke."

"I agree with everyone else—a truce is good between neighbors. It's nice to meet you. I have heard about you, too."

"I'm sure you have," she said, smiling at him. "Maybe it'll be better from now on."

They saw pictures of the new arena, the box seats on the ground floor where spectators could be close to the action, the plush suites with walls of glass at the top, plus a cantina with a seating capacity of two hundred that had food service, bars and elegant, comfortable seats with wide screens to also view the action. She saw pictures of the horse stalls and then more shots of another large area outside with seats around an adjoining outdoor arena.

The arena board chairman, John Smith, was master of ceremonies and stood to talk about the arena. He was obviously proud of the strides they'd already made. They were booked solid with horse shows, rodeo events and bull riding.

Finally, in closing, the speaker thanked all the

people attending the dinner who had contributed to building the arena and in particular thanked the three of the largest monetary contributors: Wade, Jake and Luke. As they read more names, Jake became antsy, thinking of how badly he wanted to get Claire out of here and into his arms.

It seemed like hours but was actually only half past ten when they arrived at Jake's Dallas condo. Claire's heart drummed with eagerness, because all evening she had been looking at Jake and imagining herself here with him, away from prying eyes. But she knew what this was. Jake always had moved on from the previous women he'd dated, and she didn't expect him to change. But she wanted this night with him.

"Jake, this is marvelous," she said, stepping into his entryway and seeing the big living room with two walls of glass that offered a spectacular view of the lights of Dallas at night. "Oh my word, what a view."

"I heartily agree," he said. His voice was deep with that rasp he got when he was aroused, and she turned to see him watching her as he unbuttoned his shirt. He had already shed his coat and tie, and her pulse jumped, her heartbeat racing because it was clear what he wanted.

Watching her, he crossed the room to her, tossing his shirt and then undershirt on a chair.

"My, that was fast," she said, thinking about his handsome looks. Then she sighed under her breath and whispered only to herself, "Ahh, Jake. You're going to have my heart." She slipped her arm around his waist as he reached out to slide his hand to her collar.

"I knew this would zip down the front. I do like your dress," he said, watching her as he pulled the zipper down slowly.

"Oh, darlin', are you gorgeous," he said, his gaze going to her breasts in a bra that was only a bit of white lace. "So incredibly beautiful," he added, letting her dress come open. She wore white lace panties that were as skimpy as her bra.

In seconds the silk dress fell around her ankles, and she stepped out of it, removing her bra and panties as he watched. He shed the rest of his clothes while he watched her.

He slipped his arms around her and drew her against his warm, naked body as he leaned down to kiss her. "You're fantastic," he whispered, and then his mouth was on hers and she clung tightly to him.

"I can't wait this time. Next time will be for you," he said after a moment and picked her up. "Put your legs around me."

When she did, he lowered her on his hard manhood and she closed her eyes, gasping with pleasure as he eased into her slowly.

"Ahh, Jake," she whispered, clinging to him and moving with him, each thrust sending waves of intense pleasure that rocked her.

As she clung tightly to him, he began to pump

faster. Sensations spread in her, desire hot and intense as she rode him and tension built. She felt her first climax burst with a fantastic surge, ecstasy enveloping her. He continued pumping faster, and in minutes she clutched him, clinging with her arms and legs tight around him as her second climax washed over her while he climaxed at the same time. She cried out while spasms racked her, and then she fell on him, kissing him and holding him tightly until she finally slid down to stand on the floor again while they still kissed.

He picked her up to carry her to bed, stretching out on his side and holding her close as she faced him. "Jake, I can't move now. You're fantastic."

"I guarantee you, that's my line. You looked beautiful tonight, in your clothes and out of them. Absolutely stunning."

She smiled at him, running her fingers over his whiskers, along his ear, up into his hair. "I think when I move out of your house, my heart may just be left behind with you. Probably another trophy for you."

"I don't have trophies like that or women like that in my life," he said as he looked deeply into her eyes. "I don't know about the future, but I know that right now, I'm in paradise because of you."

"I could say the same thing."

He held her close against him. "This is good."

She clung tightly to him, happy, refusing to think

beyond the current moment. She'd had a fabulous evening, and Jake's response to her new clothes, her new haircut and style, had been more than she had hoped for. She knew some rough times lay ahead, because it was inevitable that she would move out of his house and into her new one, but right now, tonight, she wasn't going to think again about anything beyond the moment. And at the moment, she was euphoric. They'd shared hot lovemaking. She was being held tightly against his naked body and in due time he would kiss her again and they would make love again. It was paradise now while she was naked in his arms. She wouldn't look beyond the immediate moment.

With a sigh, she hugged him tightly and put her head on his chest to listen to his heartbeat.

"This is the perfect end to a perfect day," he said, his voice a deep rumble. She could feel vibrations in his chest when he talked. She ran her fingers over his flat, hard stomach, sliding them up over his chest. "You're incredible, so sexy, so handsome, so exciting," she whispered, wondering if she was already deeply in love with him and if he was going to break her heart when they said goodbye. She had a feeling she would never again know a man who was as sexy and exciting as he.

Claire spent the next week making arrangements with all sorts of people, and by the beginning of

March, her land had been cleared and a foundation laid for her new home. She went back and forth from Jake's cabin each day in one of his pickups and then usually stayed at Jake's in the afternoon. She spent every night and some days and afternoons in his bed in his arms, and she refused to think about the future unless she had to, and then only regarding her property.

Late in the day on a Thursday, she knew Jake was working on something in his office. She had been on the phone with her insurance agent and had an appointment set. She had spent the morning selecting tile and wallpaper and flooring for her new kitchen on the ranch.

After three in the afternoon, she was ready for a break and went to Jake's library. Wearing new jeans, new sneakers and a new blue T-shirt her own size, she was thankful to have some new clothes. Idly, she roamed around the room, looking at a large collection of books of all genres.

She glanced down on a lower shelf and saw a small scrapbook. She pulled it off the shelf and saw it was Jake's baby book. Smiling, she sat on the floor to look at it. When she finished, she replaced it and looked at the other books.

On the bottom shelf, she noticed what looked like another scrapbook pushed back where it was almost hidden by books. She pulled it out to look at pictures of Jake when he was in high school. As she closed it to put it back where she found it, a couple of pictures fell out.

She picked them up and looked at a picture of a family—a tall, slender, balding man, a woman who had short, straight brown hair and a big smile. There were four kids, two girls and two boys. The tallest boy looked anywhere from sixteen to eighteen. The others ranged in ages from that to the youngest girl, who looked five or six. Claire wondered who they were. Probably relatives of Jake's, she assumed. More Reeds who didn't live in this area.

She put the picture back and started to move on to the next thing, but she stopped. Something had looked vaguely familiar about the woman. She picked up the picture again to stare at it intently while her heart beat faster. She placed her finger over the woman's hair to just look at her face only.

Claire suddenly felt frozen, as if she was in ice water.

Ten

She stared at the picture, and the chill she felt deepened, making her shake. And then her icy feelings began to change, her temperature climbing as shock changed to fury.

She was certain she was looking at a picture of her sister. Her hair was different, and she was heavier and older, but it had to be Regina. Regina and Jake's brother, Sam, and their family.

As she held the picture and stood, Claire shook with anger. The scrapbook fell from her lap, hitting the floor with a clatter, but she didn't even notice.

She stared at the picture in her hand again. It couldn't have been more than a year or two old for

Regina to have a son taller than she was and looking at least sixteen or older. Jake had contact with Regina and his brother. He had a picture of them and their family, so he had to have been in contact. And not that long ago.

She thought of the intimacy she had shared with Jake, sharing her feelings, her body, her hopes, her fears, even her heart. And all the time he had known where his brother and her sister were. He had known about their family. He had to have known and had to have been in touch with them to get this picture.

Regina and Sam had four kids and Jake had known this—how long?

Had he known about them since they left Texas?

In her memory, Claire always thought of Regina just as she had been the night she left. The woman in the picture bore little resemblance to the sister Claire remembered, but everyone changed with time.

Regina had dyed her blond hair brown, or maybe it had just turned brown, because there were a lot of gray streaks now. Her naturally curly hair had been straightened and cut very short—a style she'd never worn before she left home. That was the biggest change, plus the glasses, but those could easily be fake. Or by this time, they might be real. It was difficult to recognize her but not impossible, and Claire hurt again. She had loved Regina, always missed her and thought about her and hoped she was happy.

Claire looked at the picture again. "Regina," she said, running her finger over her sister's picture.

Sam had his arm across her shoulders. He had changed as much as Regina. The hair loss was why she just glanced at him. Sam had had thick brown hair and wore it long. Now it was thinning, leaving a bald spot on the top of his head. His hair was short, with streaks of gray. How old was the picture? It couldn't be very old.

"I've missed you so," she whispered, looking again at Regina's picture. For Regina and Sam to stay away all these years, they must have felt terribly threatened by her brothers and her dad. At the time they disappeared, they probably were right about the reaction of the men in the Blake family. She didn't want to think about what they might have done to Sam. But she knew they would have just barged in and brought Regina home.

And Jake knew where they were, had contact with them and hadn't said one word to her. Anger shook her and was as strong as the hurt she felt that he would do such a thing. He hadn't trusted her at all.

Clenching her fists, Claire trembled with rage, feeling betrayed. She had made clear to Jake how much Regina had meant to her. And he had just listened and never said a word, keeping quiet when she talked about how much she had loved her sister, how much she longed to know Regina was happy and well.

How could he have been so deceitful? How could he have held back and not shared that he knew Regina had a family?

At that moment she was so angry that she was glad he wasn't present so that she had time to pull herself together and think before she told him how she felt. It was probably something like this—some huge deceitful thing—that snowballed into the old feud they were all locked into.

She wanted to get away from Jake, away from his cabin. She couldn't go home to her ranch, because there was still no place to stay on it. She found the website for the hotel in Persimmon and booked a room.

She looked at the picture again. At the four children. Then she realized she was an aunt. Aunt Claire. She turned the picture and saw Regina's neat cursive writing: Sam Jr., Claire Lynn, Becky and Charles. Their grandfather's middle name.

"Claire Lynn," she read aloud, looking at a picture of a teenage girl with curly brown hair. "Claire Lynn," Claire repeated, certain Regina had named their first girl for her. "Aunt Claire," she said aloud, still stunned to discover the picture.

How could Jake have kept this from her? The question tore at her repeatedly as she thought about how she had poured out her heart to him about her pain and overwhelming sense of loss when Regina and Sam eloped.

She shook with anger and pain. She yanked up her phone again to make arrangements to be picked up and driven to Persimmon, where she already had a suite. She didn't want to spend one more minute with Jake than she had to.

She heard boots in the hall and looked up to see Jake standing in the doorway.

Eleven

Jake had walked down the hall looking for Claire. She could slip away from him and she was quiet, even in boots. As he'd reached the open door to the study, he'd almost walked past it, but he'd seen her seated and turned back, smiling as he'd stepped into the doorway. Now he looked at her and at an open book on her lap and a picture in her hand, and his heart sank. He had forgotten about the damn picture of her sister and her family.

"Claire—"

She shook her head. "Don't start, Jake. There isn't an explanation of any sort that will make up for you not telling me that you know where my sister is. And you've known all along." Her voice was low, tight with anger, and he felt his hurt deepen.

"I promised them I wouldn't tell anyone," he said as he entered the room and started to approach her. When she held up her hand, he paused.

"Stop. Don't you come near me," she said.

"I promised I wouldn't tell anyone," he repeated with an emphasis on the last word. "If I had told you, I would have broken my promise to my brother and to her. I couldn't. I had to keep my promise to them."

A tear spilled down Claire's cheek, and she hastily wiped it away with the back of her hand, and he felt worse. He could see the anger blazing in her green eyes.

"There's nothing you can ever say to make keeping this from me right. I've given you my body. Unfortunately, I probably gave you part of my heart, too, but I will get over that if I haven't already. Your promise is no excuse at all. We're intimate. If you had told me, don't you think I could have kept quiet about it?"

"I don't know. Would you have kept quiet? Or would you want to contact Regina? I think you'd want to talk to her and maybe go see her. I don't see them. They severed relations with everyone here except me. My brother has kept in touch. He makes the contact—I don't. He's never come to see me."

"Have you gone to see him?"

"Yes, four times, after the birth of each of their

kids. They invited me to come, so I went. He doesn't come back here. It's your family that drove them away. Mine is bad, but your dad and your brothers are worse. I know Regina wanted to contact you, but your two older brothers and your dad kept her away. She was afraid they would find out. She was afraid of what they might do."

"Jake, there's nothing you'll ever be able to say to make it right or for me to forgive you," she said.

"This is tearing me up. I don't want to hurt you even the tiniest bit."

"Oh, please. Stop, Jake. You kept Regina's whereabouts, information about her and her family, secret from me while we were intimate. When I leave here, I never want to see you again."

"Look, give me a chance here—"

"When I gave you my body, I also gave you my trust. And I expected it to be mutual. Well, it quite obviously was not." She shook her straight red hair back from her face.

"Look, I'm sorry. I did what I thought was best for them."

"Just stop. I've already called for a driver to come here and pick me up. I said I would be by the gate because I know you value your privacy."

"Cancel that and let me take you to Dallas or wherever you want to go," he said, hurting, wishing he could undo what had happened. "I forgot that damn picture—"

"How long ago was it taken?"

"A year ago. They're all a year older now. Claire, they're not coming back. They don't communicate except my brother has let me know when a baby is born."

"How close were you with your brother?"

"Close enough," he answered. "They're scared of your dad and your brothers. And probably rightfully so at first. By now, your dad is older, your brothers are scattered and have other interests. All of them are accustomed to Regina's disappearance, and if she returned, none of you would live under the same roof again, so it's all different now. When Sam and Regina left, they had justification for secrecy."

"I know they did, but it's years later now, as you just said. You could have told me without any repercussions to them. I wouldn't have jumped on a plane and gone to see her or even called her. It just hurts to know that you have no trust in me. It hurts that you kept something so important from me. At least you made it quite clear where I stand with you and how deep your feelings go for me and how much you trust me. I'm leaving, and I don't want to see you again ever."

"I know you have appointments about your house, and you'll need to be out here where you can meet with people and look at the damage, so just stay here and I'll keep out of your way."

"Thank you, but no. I got a suite at the hotel in

Persimmon. They had one available, and I can drive back and forth from there, so I don't need to stay here. And I don't want to stay with you one minute longer than I have to. I do not want to see you again," she said slowly and firmly.

With each word, his hurt deepened, and finally he felt a twinge of anger because she wouldn't listen, wouldn't accept his apology, wouldn't give him a chance. If she was so hell-bent on being let in on the secret about her sister, maybe he should just throw the other family secret at her.

"I'll get my things," she said and turned to start out of the room.

"All right, Claire," he said. "You want me to share family secrets with you that concern you," he said, anger and hurt overcoming his judgment. She stopped walking, turned and frowned, staring at him.

"Do you want me to share another big family secret with you? One you can't tell anyone else and I've never told anyone. I'll be happy to trust you with it."

She crossed her arms over her chest and continued to stare at him. "Okay, Jake, what is it?"

"Here's another one about your family and mine. That third brother of yours. His mother is your mother...but his dad is my father."

"Laird?" Her eyes widened, and she looked stunned.

"Yes, Laird. And he might not know this—he didn't when I was told. His mother is your mother, as everybody thinks, but his dad is my dad, not yours. My dad thought I should know that we're related and both of us are his sons. He didn't tell me until I was older. That's why there was such bitterness and active fighting between our dads and our grandfathers, because all four of them knew the truth."

"Laird is only my half brother?"

"Yes, Laird is half brother to both of us."

She barely heard his answer. Her mind reeled with all the shocks—Regina, Laird—and the pain of Jake's betrayal. That hurt overwhelmed her, and she realized she had fallen in love with Jake or she wouldn't be feeling so hurt by him. She was hurt by what he did, and she was hurt because she would never go out with him again. That was incredible pain, and it meant she was deeply in love with him. She tried to push away the thought and listen, because he was still talking to her.

"…and Laird and I are friends. Now are you happier that you know that secret?"

"That's different from knowing about Regina. That secret about Laird does explain why there was such animosity with our dads. And maybe why Laird is different from my other brothers. Otherwise, that information has little to do with me."

He stared at her and knew there wasn't any fixing their broken relationship, and that hurt. He had never hurt over losing a woman before, but now he felt physical pain. He hadn't intended to hurt her, and he regretted keeping the picture. He wished he could go back and live some moments over to undo the pain he had caused her.

As Claire walked away, she dropped the picture, letting it fall to the floor. She passed him without looking at him and hurried down the hall to get her things. The driver would be at the gate before she could possibly get there.

She had only a few things to pack. When she was ready to go, Jake stood in the doorway.

"I told you to leave me alone."

"Let me drive you to the gate. That's a damn long walk."

"Very well," she said, nodding and knowing he was right. She should have told the driver to pick her up at his cabin. "I don't have much to carry."

She walked to the door, and he followed her into the hall. They walked in silence to his pickup, and he held the door for her. Hurting, fighting tears and still steeped in anger, she climbed in and didn't look at him. As she thought how badly she hurt, she realized this might be the last time she saw Jake.

Maybe her anger with him would help her get over him.

Jake got in, and as he drove, they were both silent. She'd said all she wanted to say to him, and truthfully, she couldn't wait to get away from him. She hurt all over. She felt angry, betrayed and in pain.

Her heart ached. She didn't want to admit that she had fallen in love with him, but she knew she had. How could she have avoided it after their first kiss? It was going to hurt terribly at first to leave him and not see him anymore, but she couldn't stay. Besides, she told herself, she'd always known this day would come sometime anyway.

Trying to get her thoughts off Jake, she thought about what he had told her about Laird. She rarely saw Laird now that they were grown, and they weren't close at all when they were together. Even so, it was still a shock, but it was a possible explanation for why Laird wasn't like her other two brothers. Her mother had had an affair with Jake's dad in spite of the strong feud. She was surprised there hadn't been bigger battles between the dads and between the families, but her mother had her own money, was very independent and had kept a reasonable amount of peace in the family when she was alive.

Then she thought about her sister. Regina had four kids. The oldest one looked almost eighteen. A girl named for her. Claire. She was Aunt Claire. She felt another stabbing pain of longing to meet these children who were related to her. She longed to talk to Regina, just briefly. If Jake had told her about Sam and Regina, would she have been able to promise not to contact Regina?

She didn't want to answer her own question because it didn't matter now. She still didn't know where Regina was, and Jake wasn't going to tell her.

She could understand why Regina had severed ties. Clyde, Les and her dad had been capable of doing real damage to someone if they were angry enough. But as worried she was that they might have even done something to Jake, too, that wouldn't be true now. They were all older. Her dad had probably stopped his fighting long ago because of being older and not well. He wouldn't fight over Laird now at all. The last time she saw her dad, he'd had a cane and an eye patch, and he looked frail.

As rotten as they could be, her brothers had jobs and businesses they started, and she couldn't imagine them fighting now, because now they had too much to lose. They were successful businessmen, Clyde in real estate and Les in construction but she suspected they didn't worry much about ethics.

She stared out the window. Every mile took her away from Jake. She wouldn't see him again, wouldn't talk to him or be with him again. They wouldn't kiss again. That hurt, but she couldn't stay with him after learning that he knew about Regina. He would have shared the truth if he had really trusted her. She wondered how long she would live with the hurt.

They reached Jake's gate, which stood open. "I'll get out here, Jake. You don't need to wait with me," she said, determined not to give in to tears. She hurt, but her anger overrode her pain. "Thank you for taking me in and for everything you did for me."

"I don't want you to go like this, Claire, but you know what you want."

She was still angry with him, shocked over his knowledge of her sister's whereabouts. At the same time, she was in love with him, and telling him goodbye was already the most painful thing she'd ever had to endure.

It had been inevitable from the outset because she'd always known they had no future together. Jake wasn't a marrying man, and she couldn't marry a Reed. She gave a sarcastic laugh to herself. That would bring her brothers and her dad back to town, for sure. But she wanted peace and harmony with her family and keeping Jake close would not be good. And now, she felt she couldn't trust him.

She wondered if the next time Jake talked to his brother if he would even tell Sam that she had found their picture and knew he was in contact with them. If he did tell Sam, would it make a difference?

She wondered, too, if Regina had missed her half as much as she missed Regina. Probably not because when Regina left, she was no doubt wrapped up in being in love with Sam and getting married. Her eleven-year-old sister wouldn't have been that big a part of her life after she left home and married. Especially if she got pregnant right away. Now she had Sam and four kids to love. Regina had probably severed ties and never looked back and figured Claire had gone on with her life, too.

Claire remembered her friend Stefanie's joy over being an aunt and what fun Stefanie had with her nieces and nephews. Stefanie got to see her nieces and nephews. Claire never had and never would. There wasn't any joy in discovering she was an aunt when she couldn't possibly see or talk to her nieces and nephews. Even if they met her now, they would have no interest in her, because they had never known her.

Pain filled her for so much that had happened in the past, but it was Jake causing the deep hurt. Regina had been gone a long time, and that hurt had dulled through the years—Claire had learned to live with it. What hurt now was telling Jake goodbye, because she had fallen in love with him. She hurt because she loved him, but if she had it to do over, she would react the same way. Jake should have told her about Regina and Sam and trusted her, which he would have if he loved her. Obviously he was not in love with her.

She had known from the start that she was going to get hurt by Jake. She'd known he wouldn't fall in love, and she had guessed that she would. Well, she had, and it hurt terribly to tell him goodbye.

She finally gave in to tears, crying, missing him already, knowing he was gone from her life. Would she ever really get over him? Could she ever forget him?

She heard a car and saw the one coming that had been described to her as her ride. Wiping her eyes, she shouldered her bag and glanced back one time in the direction of Jake's cabin. All she could see were mesquite trees scattered across the fenced fields. Jake had driven away and out of her life.

She turned as the car stopped and a driver got out to greet her and open a back door for her.

Jake drove home and sat in his car after he had parked. He stared into space, seeing Claire and thinking about her. It hurt to have her go and have her angry with him. He had never parted that way with anyone else.

He hated to part that way, and he hated that Claire had been hurt. Honestly, he hadn't thought once about that picture. He hadn't even looked at it since it came last year. But she wouldn't listen to him now. She was in shock, and maybe when the shock wore off, he could talk to her.

He had always kept his brother's secret, and he was still staying true to his promise. Sam and Regina had never contacted any of their relatives here, including Claire, so he'd just stayed true to his vow of secrecy. After all these years, he didn't give enough thought to Claire still wanting to connect with her sister—and he should have started thinking about that when they became closer and intimate. He'd made a mistake, and he wished he could fix it. But it was too late now. He suspected Claire had said goodbye to him forever.

With a sigh, he got out of his pickup and went inside. He needed to go work—tough physical work that would take his mind off Claire and enable him to get over her. He wished he could talk her out of her decision to leave, but he knew he couldn't. Her relationship with her sister had been tight, and he had a feeling Claire's feelings would never change. She'd never understand why he hadn't shared that info with her—but he had given a promise, and he kept his promises.

He swore softly. He needed to find some work that would take his mind off Claire. He needed to work straight through the night. His nights had been spent with Claire in his arms and their fabulous lovemaking. He was going to have to work himself close to passing out tonight if he hoped to get one second's sleep.

He already missed her, and that surprised and worried him. He had never missed any woman before. He hadn't been ready to say goodbye to Claire. He couldn't recall any time a woman had walked away when he wasn't ready to see her go. But he wasn't ready with Claire.

"Damn," he said quietly. He already missed her, and she had just gotten out of his sight. He went to get some tools. He had some jobs he had put off doing, and now was a good time because they were demanding, physical jobs that would tire him out and take his mind off Claire.

He told himself he'd get over her soon, because he hadn't known her long enough to be deeply serious. What he needed was time and to keep busy and to go out with someone really fun who could occupy his mind.

She wasn't that important to him.

But he couldn't ignore that nagging voice inside his head that repeated the same question over and over again. *If she isn't, why do you hurt so badly?*

He changed clothes, got tools and drove out to an area where cedars had taken root. Even a little cedar was a chore to dig up and get rid of, but hard work was exactly what he needed.

Jake began to dig, working furiously, determined to get Claire out of his thoughts.

It was dark when he returned to his dim, empty house. He went to his gym to work out and run on a treadmill. He hoped to work off some of his worries and also to try to reach a point where he might sleep a little tonight.

He finally showered, dressed in jeans and a T-shirt and went to the kitchen to get dinner, but nothing sounded good—he wasn't hungry, and he missed Claire more than he would have thought possible.

Instead of dinner, he reached for a beer. As he sat

at the table with it, he took out his small directory of phone numbers and addresses and looked for his brother's. He sat there for twenty minutes debating whether to make the call. Then finally he picked up his phone and called Sam.

Claire sat in the empty hotel room. She had cried until she thought she couldn't possibly have any more tears left. And then she cried again. She cried over Jake, over her sister, over the whole dang feud.

Her phone rang, and her pulse jumped. It beat even faster when she saw that the call was from Jake.

Her heartbeat raced faster when she answered and heard his deep voice. "Claire, it's Jake. I've talked to Sam," he said, talking fast. "I called to tell him about you and that you found their picture, so I had to tell you a few things."

Shocked, she listened. She hadn't thought about what Jake might do because she was too busy sobbing, missing him and wishing she was with him. How deeply in love with him was she?

"Claire? Are you still there?"

"I'm here," she replied.

"Regina wants you to call them. They were going to call you, but they thought they might have trouble getting through and you would have a better chance. You can FaceTime them or you can just phone. Your choice. That's straight from Regina. When you're ready, I'll tell you the number."

She was amazed. When she could finally formulate the words, she said, "Jake, thank you. Go ahead. What's her number?"

She listened and wrote down the number on the hotel pad. Her heart raced over getting to call Regina, over Regina wanting her to call and over Jake doing this for her.

"Jake, thank you," she said again. She missed him, wished she had handled things a little differently, but she was still too deeply hurt that he hadn't confided in her. "I'll call Regina now."

"Good luck. It's good to hear your voice. I miss you." His voice grew thick with emotion and then he cleared his throat. "Go on and give her a call."

"I will right now. Thanks," she said, reluctant to break the connection with him, yet knowing it was over between them. She just didn't think she'd ever be able to get past his lack of trust in her. His deception. Besides, she told herself, they wouldn't have had a future together anyway because of the old feud. There was no way she would lose her connections with her family.

Regina had lived all these years cut off from the family members she loved. Jake's brother had lived cut off from his family and from Jake. She didn't want that. Even if Jake got down on his knee and proposed and offered her a ring, she would have to say no.

She didn't want to live cut off from the relatives she loved the way Regina had.

She ended the call with him and punched in the telephone number Jake had given her. In seconds, she couldn't believe it—she was talking to her sister and looking at her. "Regina, I've missed you so much. I'm going to cry, and I can't help it. You look wonderful, and you have a family. I want to see them."

"Jake told us about the fire. I've missed you so, but it seemed best just to sever the ties. I didn't want to take a chance on Dad or our brothers discovering you knew where we are. They would have ruined your life until you told them. I love you too much to allow that to happen."

Her sister wiped at the tears in her eyes. Regina might look different, but the minute they started talking, Claire recognized the sister that she loved. "I'm sorry if that was wrong, Claire. Actually, part of it is still thinking of you as my little sis and so young, which is silly. You grew up just like I did. I'll send you a ticket if you can fly out here and visit us before you start getting all involved in building a new ranch house. Can you come visit?"

"Oh yes," she said, crying with joy and excitement. "I'd love to see all of you. I can come as soon as I can make flight arrangements. But you don't need to get my ticket. I'll get it."

"I should have contacted you, but when I left, you were a little girl, and I didn't think it would be a good idea to call you. If our dad had discovered we were talking, he might have used you to force me to come home. He would have wrung out of you how to get in touch with me if you had known. I was afraid you'd get hurt trying to protect me. Then as the years went by, I just let it go." Regina ran a hand through her short hair. "I still love you, Claire, and I still miss you. Don't think I ever stopped loving you or missing you."

"Oh, Regina, I understand. You were probably right to protect me at that age."

They talked for an hour, and after that Claire spoke to each of the children, getting to know them a little. She couldn't believe the oldest was almost out of high school. When they finally said goodbye, Claire smiled and threw her arms in the air. She wanted to celebrate—with Jake. Then, her smile faded.

Jake wasn't part of her life anymore. And she'd better get used to it.

But ironically, if it weren't for Jake, she wouldn't be back in touch with her sister, nor would she be going to see Regina. She had to at least call and thank him for that.

For right now she pushed aside thoughts about him. She had something more pressing to do: she needed to get her plane ticket and make arrangements to go visit Regina. After all these years, she couldn't wait.

* * *

It had been so long since he saw her last. Jake knew Claire had gone to see her sister. She had called him before she left, sounding incredibly happy about the trip. He had called Sam and Regina and talked to Claire several times since she'd gone to visit them. Now she was coming home tomorrow and he ached to see her, to hear about her trip.

He had missed her more than he had ever missed any woman. He thought about her all through his waking hours, and he was making mistakes because his thoughts would drift to Claire and he would forget what he was doing.

He got up on the weekend and cooked breakfast for himself, putting strips of bacon in his big iron skillet. He turned the fire low on his gas range and then turned to get orange juice. He glanced out the window and saw his back gate was open. His big Lab knew how to open the gate and frequently did. Then the dog would go join the cowboys and spend the day around them. The dog had figured out how to open the gate, but he never tried to learn how to close it, despite the countless times Jake had tried to teach him. Jake went out to close it, because the dog could open it and get back in if he wanted to.

Jake gazed at the horizon and thought about the past month. He still missed Claire and wanted to see her as soon as she returned from visiting her sister. Maybe she was over being mad at him. She had sounded happy the last time they talked and actually she told him she missed him. Feeling hopeful for the first time in a long time, he turned to go back to the kitchen and glanced at the window.

Orange flames flickered, and he remembered his bacon in the big skillet. He ran back inside, grabbing a fire extinguisher as he ran through the back entryway.

When he raced into the kitchen, a fire burned in the skillet and had caught a curtain at the window. That's what he had seen burning.

He turned off the gas burner and then raised the extinguisher, aiming it at the curtain, squirting it and putting out the fire in seconds. Next, he grabbed a lid for the iron skillet, covered it and smothered that fire. Taking a deep breath, he pulled out a chair and sat down at the table. That all had happened because he couldn't keep from thinking about Claire.

There was no more denying it. He was in love with her. For the first time in his life, he was in love. He wanted her back in his life. He wanted her in his life all the time.

Would she ever get over her anger with him? She had said she missed him. How strong were her feelings for him? Could he ever get her back?

He thought about the feud and her feelings about that. She had repeatedly told him they could never have a permanent relationship even if they ever wanted one because of the feud. She had said she never wanted to marry and be cut off from her family the way Regina had been. That damned old feud! It was time to end it. He stared into space, racking his brain for any way possible to bring it to a conclusion. Would anyone be willing to join him and let the feud die?

Then he thought about Claire again. When he saw her again, would he be able to persuade her to take a chance on marriage? Did he really want to marry at this point in his life? It was years sooner than he had ever expected to settle down.

He had always thought he would marry when he was in his forties. He hadn't ever wanted to be tied down before that.

He remembered that night they'd lain in bed when he'd told her that his time with her had been paradise. Such true words. He leaned over the table and thought about his life and about Claire. No matter what age he was now, he wanted her back. He missed her. He loved her and he wanted—needed—her in his life. He was ready to settle down with her... but could he ever talk her into marriage? She was a strong person, accustomed to running her life and making her decisions alone. Could he convince her to take a chance on marrying him?

He didn't even know for certain if she was over her anger with him about Regina.

There was a way to get answers to all his questions if he really wanted to. He took a deep breath and began to make plans. The problem that loomed first might be the next to the biggest one—could he get her to see him?

Twelve

It had been a week since Claire arrived back in Dallas and then drove out to Persimmon to move back into the hotel suite. She'd had a wonderful time with Regina and her family, and for a couple of days she was in euphoria from her trip and being with her sister, but that had worn off. She was home now, and she missed Jake. She had gotten along at her sister's because she was so busy with Regina and her family, but since the first solitary night in Dallas and then the next night in Persimmon by herself, she'd missed Jake badly. It surprised her how much she missed him.

She was the one who'd told him goodbye, who'd

told him to get out of her life, but now it was a void she didn't like. She missed him in too many ways—his sexy kisses and lovemaking, his upbeat outlook, his companionship, his flirting and constant light touches that built desire but also made her aware that he liked being with her.

How many times a day did she reach for her phone to call him, then stop? He would walk out of her life at some point anyway. The more he was in her life before he said goodbye, the more she would hurt when he left.

At least that was what she told herself, but it wasn't working out well. No matter what argument she used, she still missed him and wanted to be with him.

Could she really take him back in her life when it might just mean more heartache later? She may have changed, but it didn't necessarily mean Jake had. He wasn't a marrying man—he'd told her that upfront—so even if they made up, Jake wouldn't propose. Did she want to live a life of just being with him for a time without marriage?

Even though she didn't know what was in store for their future, she knew she had already forgiven him. And, she needed to think before she called to thank him for telling his brother about her. If Jake hadn't told them, she never would have seen Regina again, and for that she was grateful.

But she needed to figure out what exactly she wanted from Jake.

She paced the suite from door to window, but she couldn't stop the questions that echoed in her head. Could she accept life on Jake's terms? Was she better off just trying to get over him?

Twenty minutes later she was still pacing. She still had no answers. All she knew was that she was wildly in love with him and she had sent him packing. How could she get him back?

Her cell phone rang, and her heart skipped a beat when she saw the call was from Jake. Smiling, she answered.

"Claire, I want to take you to dinner tomorrow night," he said.

"That's getting right to the point," she said. "I'd love to go to dinner with you tomorrow night."

"That's good. Does this mean I'm a little bit forgiven?" She could hear the tentativeness in his speech even though he tried to put it a light tone.

"Yes, you are," she answered, suddenly serious and wishing he was with her right now. "We can talk about it tomorrow night."

"Good. How about seven? And plan on a long evening. We need to talk."

"Now I'm curious," she said, wishing he had asked her for dinner tonight, because she wanted to be with him.

"Any chance we could move this dinner up to tonight?" he asked.

"You're a mind reader—even over the phone. I'd love to move it up to tonight."

"See you at seven."

"See you at seven," she answered, echoing him. She disconnected the call and felt her entire body pulsate. She was too excited to sit still and began pacing again, this time with a smile on her face instead of a frown. She needed something to wear— her sexiest dress. "Jake Reed, I'm about to make you sit up and take notice."

She couldn't wait for the day to pass. She wanted to be with him with all her being. She wanted to kiss him and be kissed, to love and be loved by him. She wanted tonight with him and to make up with him, and if he broke her heart later, she would just deal with it when it happened. She screeched and jumped in the air, throwing her arms up and twirling around. "Jake, I'm going to love you tonight until you never want to let me go."

That might be a pipe dream because he always moved on, but she was going out with him tonight, and maybe, just maybe, he'd stick around awhile.

At exactly 6:59 p.m., when Claire opened the door to face Jake, she wanted to throw her arms around his neck and hug him. He wore navy slacks and a pale blue long-sleeved shirt that was unbuttoned at the collar, and he looked incredibly handsome. She smiled and greeted him.

"Come in. I'm ready. I wanted to say a few things to you before we go out."

"You look gorgeous," he said, his voice lowering a notch.

"It's a dress I don't wear often—not much need for it on the ranch, and it isn't exactly a church dress," she said, glancing down at her black sleeveless dress that had a straight skirt and a plunging neckline. She looked up at him.

"Jake, I had a long talk with Regina, and she made me see how important it was to them that you didn't tell anyone about them. She was grateful for your secrecy and made me understand. I told you I never wanted to see you again, but that's not true at all. Even when I was angry at you, I missed you so much. The thought of us not being together…" she trailed off.

Jake grabbed her hands. "The important thing is we're here now, and I'm glad. I missed you. And, I promise I won't keep something like that from you again. We're in this together now."

"I've missed you so much," she said.

He pulled her to him, his arm going around her waist as he leaned down to kiss her. She wrapped her arms around his neck, stood on tiptoe and kissed him in return, her heart racing as she lost herself in his fabulous sexy kiss.

Suddenly, he stepped away slightly, taking her hand in his. He gazed at her intently. "Claire, I know you don't think I'm the marrying type, but I think I was just waiting for the right woman. I love you, and I want to marry you. Will you marry me?"

Stunned, she stared at him. "Oh, Jake. I love you. I've loved you despite our families." She stared at him and couldn't get words. Tears stung her eyes. "I want to say yes, but I can't. We can't marry. I can't live the way Regina and Sam live."

She hurt badly. She loved him and suspected she always would, but she couldn't see any way they could marry. "We have that feud, and you know what that means."

He framed her face with his hands. "Listen to me. I've talked this over with Sam. We both think it's time to end that old feud. What I think we should do is have a big church wedding and invite both families."

"Oh, Jake," she said, shaking her head and wiping her eyes before the tears could fall. "My brothers—I can't imagine what they would do."

"I'll tell you what they'll do," he said. He placed his hands on her shoulders. "I've already had a talk with Clyde with Les. I took the Persimmon sheriff with me, but he stayed in the waiting rooms of their respective offices until I finished talking to them first, and then I called him in, and he talked to them. We're not going to have any trouble from Clyde or Les. I didn't bother talking to Laird, because I don't think he ever was the cause of trouble."

"I don't think so, either," she responded. But she couldn't get her mind around everything he'd said. "You talked to my brothers?"

"I did. They're businessmen now, and they don't want to get in trouble with the law or with their customers. They don't scare me, and they never have. They may have given us trouble in the past, but they won't now. Clyde has his own real estate company, and Les is a builder, and they're both doing well. They are definitely interested in keeping things that way. They won't give anybody any trouble. We have an understanding."

"Jake, they can be so sneaky—"

"So can I. They don't want trouble, believe me. Don't worry about your brothers. You'll see."

"They're not the only ones who live by that feud. A lot of the older people have strong feelings about it."

"Sam and I talked about that. That's why he and Regina and their family will come. They will be present with their four kids. Those four kids are Reeds and they are Blakes—they have both families' blood in their veins. They have relatives in both clans, and Regina is going to contact some of the Blakes and let them meet her kids, and Sam is going to contact some of the Reeds and let them meet the kids. Maybe then everyone will see how ridiculous this old feud is."

"I hadn't thought about the kids. And I never even considered that Regina and Sam would come here."

"Now back to what's important. In case you forgot, I asked you if you'd marry me, and I've told you we can work things out and stay right here in Dallas and on our ranches. So, Claire Blake, will you marry me and become Mrs. Jake Reed?"

She stared at him. "Oh yes! Yes, I will. I love you, Jake, with all my heart," she said, smiling and standing on tiptoe to throw her arms around his neck and kiss him while joy bubbled in her.

Instantly, his arm banded her waist, and he pulled her tightly against him as he leaned down to kiss her.

"Ahh, darlin', how I've missed you."

"I missed you, Jake," she whispered, and then he kissed her again. She didn't know how long they stood there in each other's embrace, bodies pressed against each other, lips together. Her heart raced with happiness. She was going to accept his offer—all of it. She would marry him, and she would stop worrying about the feud. Jake would have to work miracles to make the feud go away, but this would be a start. It might be a very big start.

Sam and Regina's kids might make a giant difference in how people felt about the feud.

When she finally could think clearly about more than the feud, she pulled back and looked up at him. "Are we still going to run two separate ranches?"

"We'll do whatever you want to do," he answered. "I'm open for anything as long as you're in my bed at night."

She laughed and put her arms around his neck again. "We'll have fun, Jake," she said.

"Hey, wait. I forgot—I didn't do this right. I brought you a present." He reached into his hip pocket and brought out a box tied with a pink ribbon. "I got this for you."

She took it from him and unfastened the bow. Her heart raced because she was filled with happiness. She was going to marry Jake, the man she loved, and she would get to keep her ranch. And maybe the sister she loved would be back in her life now.

She removed the wrapping paper and held a small box in her hand. She opened it and gasped. "Oh, Jake," she said, looking at a dazzling emerald-cut diamond.

"I did it backward. I was going to give you that, and when you opened it, then I intended to ask you if you'd marry me."

"Yes, Jake Reed, I will marry you and love you all the rest of my life," she said, looking at the dazzling big diamond and then up at the man who dazzled her far more. "I love you, Jake," she said, meaning it. Then a thought struck her. "We haven't even talked about kids. Do you want kids?"

"Yes, I do. Do you?"

"Yes, I want your kids. I don't care how many. We can decide that as we go."

He laughed and took the ring from her and held

her hand. "I'll do this right. I love you, Claire. Will you marry me?"

"Yes, Jake. I love you, and I'll marry you."

He slipped the ring on her finger and drew her to him to kiss her again. When he released her, he picked up her hand to look at the ring.

Her gaze followed his. "It's gorgeous and it fits."

"Ah, darlin', how I love you," he said, wrapping his arms around her and drawing her to him to kiss her. She kissed him in return while her heart beat fast with joy and love. She opened her eyes, waved her fingers and looked at the dazzling diamond that would always be a symbol of Jake's love. "I'm marrying the sexiest, best-looking guy in all of Texas," she said, smiling at him and hugging him.

"I want to spend a lifetime making you happy," he whispered, showering light kisses on her. "It'll be good. I promise I'll do everything I can to try to make you happy. And you know how well I keep my promises." He looked at her, and they both smiled. "I love you, darlin'."

"I love you, Jake," she said. Joy filled her, and she held him tightly, this rancher who loved the same things she did—and what was most wonderful, he had fallen in love with her. Life was wonderful.

* * * * *

Don't miss any of the stories in
The Return of the Texas Heirs series
from USA TODAY *bestselling author*
Sara Orwig

In Bed with the Rancher
One Wild Texas Night
and two more stories coming in 2021!

WE HOPE YOU ENJOYED
THIS BOOK FROM

⊕ HARLEQUIN
DESIRE

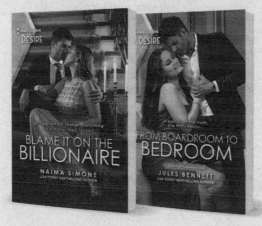

*Luxury, scandal, desire—welcome to
the lives of the American elite.*

Be transported to the worlds of oil barons, family dynasties,
moguls and celebrities. Get ready for juicy plot twists,
delicious sensuality and intriguing scandal.

6 NEW BOOKS AVAILABLE EVERY MONTH!

HDHALO2020

#2761 BILLIONAIRE BEHIND THE MASK
Texas Cattleman's Club: Rags to Riches
by Andrea Laurence

A Cinderella makeover for busy chef Lauren Roberts leads to an unforgettable night of passion with a masked stranger—commanding CEO Sutton Wingate. But when the masks come off and startling truths are revealed, can these two find happily-ever-after?

#2762 UNTAMED PASSION
Dynasties: Seven Sins • by Cat Schield

After one mind-blowing night together, bad boy photographer Oliver Lowell never expected to see Sammi Guzman again. Now she's pregnant. Passion has never been their problem, but can this black sheep tame his demons for a future together?

#2763 TEMPTATION AT CHRISTMAS
by Maureen Child

Their divorce papers were never filed! So, Mia Harper tracks down her still-husband, Sam Buchanan, aboard his luxury cruise liner. Two weeks at sea tempts them into a hot holiday affair...or will it become something more?

#2764 HIGH SOCIETY SECRETS
The Sterling Wives • by Karen Booth

Star architect Clay Morgan knows betrayal. Now he keeps his feelings—and beautiful women—at bay. Until he meets his new office manager, Astrid Sterling. Their sizzling chemistry is undeniable, but will a secret from her past destroy everything they've built?

#2765 THE DEVIL'S BARGAIN
Bad Billionaires • by Kira Sinclair

The last person Genevieve Reilly should want is charming jewelry thief Finn DeLuca—even though he's the father of her son. But desire still draws her to him. And when old enemies resurface, maybe Finn is exactly the kind of bad billionaire she needs...

#2766 AFTER HOURS REDEMPTION
404 Sound • by Kianna Alexander

A tempting new music venture reunites songwriter Eden Voss with her ex-boyfriend record-label executive Blaine Woodson. He wronged her in the past, so they vow to keep things strictly business this time. But there is nothing professional about the heat still between them...

---

*A tempting new music venture reunites songwriter
Eden Voss with ex-boyfriend Blaine Woodson, a record
label executive. He wronged her in the past, so they vow
to keep things strictly business this time. But there is
nothing professional about the heat still between them...*

Read on for a sneak peek at
After Hours Redemption *by Kianna Alexander.*

Singing through the opening verse, she could feel the smile
coming over her face. Singing gave her a special kind of joy, a
feeling she didn't get from anything else. There was nothing quite
like opening her mouth and letting her voice soar.

She was rounding the second chorus when she noticed Blaine
standing in the open door to the booth. Surprised, and a bit
embarrassed, she stopped midnote.

His face filled with earnest admiration, he spoke into the
awkward silence. "Please, Eden. Don't stop."

Heat flared in her chest, and she could feel it rising into her
cheeks. "Blaine, I…"

"It's been so long since I've heard you sing." He took a step
closer. "I don't want it to be over yet."

Swallowing her nervousness, she picked up where she'd left
off. Now that he was in the room, the lyrics, about a secret romance
between two people with plenty of baggage, suddenly seemed
much more potent.

And personal.

Suddenly, this song, which she often sang in the shower or
while driving, simply because she found it catchy, became almost
autobiographical. Under the intense, watchful gaze of the man
she'd once loved, every word took on new meaning.

She sang the song to the end, then eased her fingertips away
from the keys.

Blaine burst into applause. "You've still got it, Eden."

"Thank you," she said, her tone softer than she'd intended. She looked away, reeling from the intimacy of the moment. Having him as a spectator to her impassioned singing felt too familiar, too reminiscent of a time she'd fought hard to forget.

"I'm not just gassing you up, either." His tone quiet, almost reverent, he took a few slow steps until he was right next to her. "I hear singing all day, every day. But I've never, ever come across another voice like yours."

She sucked in a breath, and his rich, woodsy cologne flooded her senses, threatening to undo her. Blowing the breath out, she struggled to find words to articulate her feelings. "I appreciate the compliment, Blaine. I really do. But…"

"But what?" He watched her intently. "Is something wrong?"

She tucked in her bottom lip. *How can I tell him that being this close to him ruins my concentration? That I can't focus on my work because all I want to do is climb him like a tree?*

"Eden?"

"I'm fine." She shifted on the stool, angling her face away from him in hopes that she might regain some of her faculties. His physical size, combined with his overt masculine energy, seemed to fill the space around her, making the booth feel even smaller than it actually was.

He reached out, his fingertips brushing lightly over her bare shoulder. "Are you sure?"

She trembled, reacting to the tingling sensation brought on by his electric touch. For a moment, she wanted him to continue, wanted to feel his kiss. Soon, though, common sense took over, and she shook her head. "Yes, Blaine. I'm positive."

Will Eden be able to maintain her resolve?

Don't miss what happens next in…
After Hours Redemption *by Kianna Alexander.*

Available October 2020 wherever
Harlequin Desire books and ebooks are sold.

Harlequin.com

HDEXP0920

Get 4 FREE REWARDS!

We'll send you 2 FREE Books plus 2 FREE Mystery Gifts.

Harlequin Desire® books transport you to the world of the American elite with juicy plot twists, delicious sensuality and intriguing scandal.

FREE
Value Over
$20

YES! Please send me 2 FREE Harlequin Desire novels and my 2 FREE gifts (gifts are worth about $10 retail). After receiving them, if I don't wish to receive any more books, I can return the shipping statement marked "cancel." If I don't cancel, I will receive 6 brand-new novels every month and be billed just $4.55 per book in the U.S. or $5.24 per book in Canada. That's a savings of at least 13% off the cover price! It's quite a bargain! Shipping and handling is just 50¢ per book in the U.S. and $1.25 per book in Canada.* I understand that accepting the 2 free books and gifts places me under no obligation to buy anything. I can always return a shipment and cancel at any time. The free books and gifts are mine to keep no matter what I decide.

225/326 HDN GNND

Name (please print)

Address   Apt. #

City   State/Province   Zip/Postal Code

Email: Please check this box ☐ if you would like to receive newsletters and promotional emails from Harlequin Enterprises ULC and its affiliates. You can unsubscribe anytime.

Mail to the **Reader Service:**
IN U.S.A.: P.O. Box 1341, Buffalo, NY 14240-8531
IN CANADA: P.O. Box 603, Fort Erie, Ontario L2A 5X3

Want to try 2 free books from another series? Call 1-800-873-8635 or visit www.ReaderService.com.

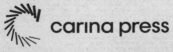